A Hoopster's Journey

The Carey Scurry Story

CAREY SCURRY

A HOOPSTER'S Journey

The Carey Scurry Story

This is a work of Non-Fiction.
A Hoopster's Journey: The Carey Scurry Story

Copyright © 2024 Carey Scurry

All rights are reserved
No part of this book may be used or reproduced in any manner whatsoever without the written permission of the copyright owner except for the use of quotations in book reviews.

ISBN: 978-1-959811-74-9 (Hardcover)
ISBN: 978-1-959811-53-4 (e-book)
Library of Congress Control Number: 2024910535

Cover Design: Okomato
Interior Design: Amit Dey
Interior Photos: From the Author's files.
Author Photo: Sam Baradie/A S Photo Cell
Editor: Marjorie Sake Winful
Co-writer: Alexander Tonico, Sports Journalist

Published in the United States by Wordeee, Beacon, New York 2024
Website: www.wordeee.com
X Formerly Twitter: wordeeeupdates
Facebook: facebook.com/wordeee/
e-mail: contact@wordeee.com

ADVANCE PRAISE

I mentored the basketball team at Long Island University in health and nutrition and taught them how to meet their potential. That was when I first met Carey; everyone could see his skills as a player. I have always believed in him, even when going through his struggles. *A Hoopster's Journey* will help him reestablish himself after his basketball career. Telling his true story in this book will help him move forward to a new chapter in his life…as well as help others.

—Idris Conroy, Former Basketball Player
President, Abu's Bakery
Bedford-Stuyvesant, Brooklyn, NY

I met Carey at Alexander Hamilton High School in Brooklyn. He was the new kid and quickly made an impression on the court. We won the championship that year…and the rest is history. He was a great guy, a great teammate, and a great friend. Reading about the highs and lows of his life's journey deeply moved me. I am totally psyched out about *A Hoopster's Journey*. Read this book!

—Jerry "Ice" Reynolds, Retired NBA Player
Milwaukee Bucks, Seattle SuperSonics,
and Orlando Magic

I met Carey Scurry through his agent, Alan Herman…and meeting Carey changed my basketball life! He was intelligent as an athlete and graceful on the court. I am from the Bronx and he's from Brooklyn. The Bronx didn't do Brooklyn and vice versa. I thought, *where did he find this guy? A Hoopster's Journey* is a true redemption story.

—Big "T" Bailey, Retired NBA Utah Jazz,
and Minnesota Timberwolves
Broadcast Analyst, Inspirational Speaker,
Singer, Songwriter and Actor

Carey was a good player and we developed a friendship. My door has always been open to him. I remember it was Carey Scurry Day in Bedford Stuyvesant in Brooklyn in 2010. He has always been great with kids. Carey was a "Gentle Giant" and his troubles with the law caught me off guard. His is a story of redemption…his heart has always been consistent and he tells his truth emphasizing that drugs can ruin your dreams in *A Hoopster's Journey*.

—Eric A. Hicks, President & CEO
Game Over Sport and Entertainment NYC
Hicks Family Foundation

I have many memories of my good friend, Carey, beginning with our playing days with the Utah Jazz organization. Cary was a great defensive player and we called him a "defensive specialist." I remember a particular story when we played against the Chicago Bulls. Michael Jordan had 40 points and the coach scanned the bench, then called out Carey to stop him. Carey said to me, "Well he already has 40 points." I responded with one of Cary's favorite lines, "Cut your odds and take a loss." We laughed many times over the years about that story and *A Hoopster's Journey* tells it all.

—Rickey Green, NBA retired
Former NBA Player, Jazz, 76ers, Boston Celtics.

FOREWORD

In the annals of NBA history, certain names etch themselves into the collective memory, not only for their athletic prowess but for the human stories their lives represent. Carey Scurry is one such name. As I sit down to pen this foreword for *A Hoopster's Journey: The Carey Scurry Story*, I am struck not only by the gravity of Carey's journey but by the resilience and courage that defines it.

I've been working with Carey for over two years now reviewing his history and speaking to his former teammates, family, and friends in preparation for this book, and yet it feels as though I've traversed lifetimes alongside him. His story is not merely a chronicle of fame and fortune, nor is it solely a tale of despair and downfall, it is, at its core, a testament to the enduring power of the human spirit, the capacity for transformation, and the unwavering commitment to redemption.

Carey's memoir is honest and authentic. He holds nothing back. Throughout these pages, Carey lays bare his vulnerabilities, his triumphs and his setbacks with unflinching honesty. He invites us into the inner sanctum of his soul, and on his journey growing up in poverty on the rough and tumble streets of Brooklyn's Bed-Stuy. He also takes us tooling around Europe in his gold Mercedes Benz. Warring against the demons of addiction, he details the success and the pitfalls he experienced as a professional basketball player. His memoir, *A Hoopster's Journey* is as much a cautionary tale as it is a beacon of hope. Delving into the complexities of fame, the seduction of fortune, and his spiraling into the harrowing abyss of addiction, he uses his story as a scared straight roadmap for those who could use it and to lift up those who may feel hopeless. *A Hoopster's Journey* is to me, more than anything, a story of rehabilitation, renewal, redemption, and ultimately the indomitable human spirit that triumphs over adversity. Even when reaching rock bottom, Carey never totally surrendered to despair. Instead, he embarked on a journey of self-discovery, confronting his demons head-on and emerging stronger on the other side.

As you embark on this journey alongside Carey, prepare to be shocked, moved, inspired, and ultimately transformed. From his story, we may find echoes of our own struggles, our own triumphs, and our capacity for redemption. Carey Scurry is more than a former NBA star; he is a beacon of hope in a world too often shrouded in darkness.

Carey's nonprofit, A Hoopster's Journey, has a mission to inspire inner-city youth to recognize their potential, realize their dreams, and the potential for him to fulfill a lifelong ambition to help others. Rebuilding bridges with loved ones and old friends is buoyed by his devotion and faith.

Carey's resilience is matched only by his humility. He doesn't seek absolution or pity; rather, he offers his story as a guiding light for those who find themselves ensnared in the same web of potential fame, adoration, addiction, and despair. His message is clear: no matter how far we fall, there is always a path to redemption, a chance to reclaim our humanity and rewrite the narrative of our lives.

—Patrice Samara, Author, Alphabet Kids Series
Co-Author, North Star, North Star

FROM THE AUTHOR

I became an addict long before I ever first picked up a pipe, I just wasn't active. Growing up in an environment where there is constant discrimination against people of color and willful media falsification of us as gangsters, criminals, and undesirables, my unconscious mind was steeped in, and programmed for, self-destruction. Black men in my neighborhood had to have the poker face of a survivor and we learned early on how to internalize anger, fear, and blatant discrimination. I was remiss at not paying attention to these predatory shadows hiding inside me, always waiting ready to pounce when the conditions were right.

The honesty in this book is intentional. It's harsh and even harsher for me to write, but if I have one thing left to give, I want to give hope to the brothers and sisters in these perilous environments. It's been over thirty years since my young life derailed and I want to emphasize that you must be vigilant about yours. As far as I can see not much has changed. So, keep in mind the subliminal conditioning of your environment, that attitude equals altitude and the company you keep is the sum total of who you are. And no matter what anyone tells you, education, which might seem out of vogue, is an equalizer. Had I had an education to fall back on when my career hit the skid, maybe my choices might have been different.

The Carey Scurry Story is a cautionary tale…but there will be more to tell. While I still walk this earth I am determined to reverse the narrative of my life. With hard work, I see a bright future I wish to share with the world. Because I have come to my senses, knowing that I'm a mere mortal man, I now know I must follow the rules of law internally and externally.

As I hung up my jersey and stepped away from the game one last time, in my heart I knew that beyond the cheers of the crowd and the roar of the arenas lies a deeper truth: You are the master of your universe. Don't squander this very short life away. Know that, until America does the work necessary to create a color-blind country, Black folks' stories like mine will continue.

A Hoopster's Journey is my true story. I hope you see it as one of determination, perseverance, heartbreak, drugs, abuse, rehabilitation, and achievement in the face of adversity but most of all, as a gift to those who need it including me.

Carey Scurry

TABLE OF CONTENTS

Dedication xiii
Chapter 1: First Quarter 1
Chapter 2: Second Quarter 13
Chapter 3: Racial Consciousness 24
Chapter 4: Opportunity Knocks. 37
Chapter 5: The Kidnapping 46
Halftime 56
Chapter 6: Third Quarter 71
Chapter 7: The Draft 84
Chapter 8: Money Comes and Money Goes 99
Chapter 9: Ditch Effort. 112
Chapter 10: Europe 127
Chapter 11: The Car Accident. 141

Chapter 12: When Life Shows Up 149

Chapter 13: The Mental Breakdown 173

Chapter 14: Fourth Quarter. 177

Chapter 14: The Pledge. 181

Chapter 16: Life Metaphorically Through Basketball 183

The Aftermath 187

Acknowledgements 190

DEDICATION

To my mother, Mildred

Thank you for never losing faith in me

— ONE —

FIRST QUARTER

Fame is a drug. Big money even more so. I've had a taste of both. In the sports and entertainment industry, elite celebrities are revered, and entitlement and exemption from bad behavior are common. Fascination with fame and fame's pomp and circumstance can reveal things about you, you never imagined. It did for me. If only I'd understood then that there was no better high than a cheering crowd, I wonder how my life would have turned out? Unsung and unrealized is a bitter pill for me to swallow when I had it all right there. I mean right there! My crowning glory, however, evaded me, all because I got in my own way. For a player, a crowd on its feet, when their team is dominating the court, is magical and a true high and I wish it had been enough.

Yeah, I was a player…a basketball player, and like every kid in poverty who watched their Mama struggle to feed her troops under trying circumstances and in dangerous neighborhoods, it was the answer to my prayers. I didn't set out like many with no way out, to dream the impossible dream because I never burned with a passion to play ball. However, the convergences of my life circumstances—my height 6'8", and my neighborhood, Bed-Stuy, made me see it as a way out. So, yes that's correct, basketball to me was not a way of life but a way out of my life circumstances. I wish I had remembered that too. To have been chosen as one of the elite of only two hundred and ten players in the United States to play in the NBA in 1985, I should have been honored. That was not too bad for a kid who only knew striving and starving as a way of life. In a single moment at the Madison Square Garden's draft picks, a player's social status and life could change forever but for me the story was different.

In my neighborhood striving was *the* way of life for far too many. My 'hood produced a lot of strivers desperate to get out from under the heavy weight of racial oppression for a 'seemingly' better life. Back when I was coming up, that usually meant one of two things: rap your way out or ball your way out. There was a third option, a more undesirable way: hustle your way out. I had a good jump so I chose ball. After all, I was raised in the Mecca of basketball, Brooklyn's very own Nostrand Avenue in Bedford-Stuyvesant, better known as Bed-Stuy. I say Mecca because a lot of good players came out of Brooklyn—people like Michael Jordan, Carmelo Anthony, and Taj Gibson. A lot of great artists too called Bed-Stuy home: The Notorious B.I.G., Aaliyah, Jay Z, Lil Kim, Maino, Eddie Murphy, Chris Rock, and Tracy Morgan to name a few. Brooklyn, too, was an epicenter for the civil rights movement and gave rise to Shirley Chisholm, the first woman to run for President of the United States. There were others too, Lena Horn, Jackie Robinson, Walt Whitman, and Judge Judy. Bed-Stuy produced a lot of questers on both sides of the race equation who wanted better for their lives.

The important question to ask is, are you prepared for fame and fortune? The influences of a world still mired in racial discrimination can play havoc on the minds of youths growing up in dire poverty. If you are from a challenging community, be particularly mindful because life in the margins can play tricks on the minds of success chasers who don't truly believe they belong. Insecurities, self-deprecation, the swag needed to fit in, and mental conditioning can bury demons in your psyche as shadows that lurk, always ready to pounce. Though one can transcend these barriers with the 'opportunities' allowed, be careful that you are not swapping one 'chain gang' for the next.

As one of nine children growing up poor in a single-parent household in the sixties and seventies, I overcame the odds few kids with a jump shot could. I was drafted into the National Basketball Association (NBA). As a Long Island University Black Bird's Hall of Famer and former player for the Utah Jazz and the New York Knicks, I came into the league during a crucial time: The Jordan Era. Michael "his Air-ness" Jordan was a game-changer player to ball as we all knew it. A true superstar with his wicked style, wagging tongue, baggy shorts, and his own sneakers dripped with charisma. When Micharl played he owned the court. Few players can honestly say they guarded Mike. When asked, most players respond, "As a team, we contained him."

So, yes, the greatest day of my life and probably the worst was when I became a Utah Jazz draft pick for the NBA. I'd done it. I had converted my prayers into a dream of a future filled with promise and possibilities for my family and me. I was ready to upgrade my life. Ready to claim my piece of the pie.

My mother's maiden name was Mildred Jones and after marrying my father she became Mr. Edward Scurry's wife. Even after having nine children, my mother remained a beautiful woman. A Christian woman, she was a faithful member of the Board of Williamsburg Christian Church and steered clear of drama. When she attended church, which she did regularly, Mama was always dressed in her finest clothes and hats. I remember how much she loved hats. I was always fascinated by Mama's beautiful hats.

Having eleven brothers and sisters of his own, when my dad wanted a big family she was only too happy to comply. My parents had five children in Edgefield, South Carolina. There was Clifton, Linda, Eddie Ruth, Dale (Day Day), and Paul (Poppa Nickels). Edgefield was and remains a rural area with, according to the 2010 census, 4, 750 residents. Part of the antebellum South, it was no stranger to sectionalism and the violence of racism. Yet Black folks always found ways to survive. One such, whose legacy lives on to today, was David Drake better known as "Dave the Potter." He was an enslaved African American, barred from literacy by the laws of those days. In defiance, Dave would inscribe his pottery with poetry to which he would sign his name. He left more than 40,000 pieces of pottery with his inscriptions, a proud legacy for those who struggle f for acceptance and their rightful place. Today his works sell for over $50,000.

For my parents, life for a Black family in the South was all but easy. Living and raising her children in the rural area where she was born didn't sit well with Mama. She wanted more employment opportunities for herself, better educational opportunities for her children, and as they got older, more job opportunities. So, Mama convinced my father and they decided to migrate North to Newark, where some of her family had already settled for the promise of a better life. Newark, New Jersey, is where I was born on December 4, 1962. I was named Carey (Cake Mix) and was the 6th child in the family. I was told that my father named me Cake Mix because I had the most beautiful cheeks and people always wanted to kiss them. How that translated to my father as Cake Mix is a mystery to me but it became my nickname. There would be three more Scurry children born after me, Carolyn (Gina), Moses, and Willie for a total of nine children. Yeah, nine of us. Six brothers and three sisters.

In Newark, life wasn't much easier for my dad. The best a Black man with a decent education could hope for was an odd job from time to time. In Edgefield, Dad had worked as a contract truck driver transporting whatever he was assigned to wherever it was assigned. After giving Newark a go Dad tried to convince Mama that they should go back to the South. Due to my father's inability to find decent enough work that would allow her to stay at home, and Mama refusing to go back, she decided to look for employment to ease their burden. It was easier for women to get a job and Mama worked off the books to give my pops a little help. She would clean homes and care for the elderly, only receiving pocket change for her work. Today, these workers are called Home Attendants or Home Aids and they get paid a fair wage, but in the 50s-60s that was not the case.

Mama, constantly working, was the one holding the family together. We lived in a cramped three-bedroom apartment surrounded by four hot brick walls with 25-watt bulbs. We'd use the brighter outside light to do our homework and it also helped when Mama was cooking. With her values set to be proud and independent, Mama refused handouts, welfare, or food stamps. Living up North was something my father could not bring himself to do so he would eventually move back South without us. My mom became a single mother with nine kids and she had her hands full.

Mama had learned her lessons on how to survive a hard life from my grandmother, Ruth Williams. My grandma was very religious, and I believe her deep faith helped her overcome the trials of overt discrimination while raising her kids in a period when racism amounted to pure vitriol. Racial oppression also built her resilience muscles and up North, Grandma Ruth became Mama's foundation and reinforced her strength.

With Papa gone, Mama held our family together. Father, I'd been told, was a dissolver, always doing things to cause unnecessary stress and tension within our family. People would say that his being gone was a blessing as he would destroy any chance we had for a normal life had he stayed. I often wondered what was considered a normal life, or what would have been considered normal in those times as life for us was anything but normal. Thankfully, our grandma's sister, Aunt Carrie, already established in Newark, welcomed us with open arms when Dad left. Aunt Carrie greatly helped our family to adjust to the North.

Newark, back then, was a city of about 450,000 people. It also had the largest population of impoverished Black people outside of the South. Mama continued to struggle with poverty, housing, and the abysmal education system for her children; but one thing she made sure of was to keep us as a close-knit family. She was not about to let us get caught up between the police and the community quarrels.

Like many industrial cities, Newark was beginning to see a shift in racial strife. For years, more than fifty percent of the Black population had been complaining about police brutality and mistreatment. Between late 1962 and the end of 1963, the community began to rebel. They were no longer going to take 'it' sitting down. A daughter of the South, anticipating the pushback from segregationists, Mama decided to make another strategic move to avoid what she was sure would come, and in 1967, it did come—race riots. The Newark riots were marred with armed conflict and violence that raged in the streets for over four days. It left twenty-six people dead and hundreds injured.

The scene in Newark became comparable to the Civil War with bloody conflicts between the Blacks and the police. Chaos, violence, and property damage exceeded fifty million dollars. Like the 1965 Watts Rebellion which had lasted six days, America was put on notice by Black folks. Not being used to African Americans who didn't know their place and who were waking up to civil disobedience, intensified the pushback from White America.

Staying three steps ahead for her family's safety, Mama could see the writing on the wall, and in 1963, we were on the move again. I was only one-year-old at the time, but hand-me-down stories from my brothers said we crossed states through the Holland Tunnel. They said it was fun looking out the window of Uncle Andrew's Cadillac at the family friend's truck loaded with all our possessions. Uncle Andrew, "Old Dude" as we called him, was Mama's only brother. They said Mama was silent during the ride as she pondered her family's future.

My father continued pressuring Mama to move back to the South, but Mama always refused. Uncle Andrew did his best to keep our father at bay. He made sure his nieces and nephews were safe, teaching us how to defend ourselves against any danger we would encounter in our underserved neighborhood. Shortly after we moved, my sister Carolyn (Gina) was born. My father, who'd been coming back and forth again insisted we move to the South. Mama, of course, refused. I did not see Dad much after that. By 1966, our family was well established in our home on Skillman Street in Brooklyn.

Bed-Stuy was (and still is) a hub for Black greatness. yet a place so traumatizing that people wanted to get out and here we were moving in. People were rising in social and civic consciousness and Black pride was at an all-time high as the Black Panther Party for Self-Defense gained prominence. Chapters were established in every state in America and they were becoming a formidable force. By 1968, our family had established a sense of comfort in Bed-Stuy.

I never knew anything but grit. We were always fighting for something…food, our rights as Americans—our piece of the American Pie. People were saying things were gonna get better…a change was gonna come because a Young Minister out of Georgia was making waves. Prominent Civil Rights leaders were advancing the Black cause on the non-violent front, among them the well-respected,

Martin Luther King, Jr., a Baptist Minister, and a political philosopher who won the Nobel Prize in 1964 for combating racial inequality. He was the most influential of the Civil Rights leaders and his ideology of nonviolent resistance and nonviolent civil disobedience proved to have fangs. His effectiveness in influencing the right to vote, desegregation, labor, and civil rights gains brought out the worst of an America in transition. Long watched by COINTELPRO (Counterintelligence Program conducted by the FBI that monitored and tried to derail organizations that appeared to pose a threat to the U.S., government). He'd even received an anonymous letter instigating him to commit suicide.

I was attending Elementary School #117 at the time. I was six years old and although it was more than sixty years ago, I remember April 4th, 1968, as though it was yesterday. It was one of those moments in life, so dramatic you can never forget; like the death of JFK, Bobby Kennedy, or 9/11. I was outside in the streets playing "Coco-levio," a tag game that originated right here in New York with some friends. An urgent summons ordered us all home. The news waiting for us when we got home was that Martin Luther King, Jr. had been assassinated outside a hotel room in Tennessee. The news shook my family and the entire community to the core. Though I didn't fully comprehend what all of this meant I knew something awful and life-changing had happened. I knew a Black man would always be up against the wall. For the civil rights leaders of the time, challenging the system of racial equality, their lives always hung in the balance. King's death brought a consciousness to the city as it equally sent a shiver up the spine of anyone bucking the system of racism. But King's death, for a moment, also intensified the empowerment for change.

Since the 1920s Blacks have been the majority residents of Bed-Stuy. The sprawling neighborhood even with its majestic Victorian brownstones could not stop the blight that led to race riots in 1961,

1967 and 1968. The NYPD was seen as hostile and they made life a living hell for the nearly 85% Black neighborhood. From the Black Panther's headquarters in Bed-Stuy, which was housed in an Afrocentric bookstore on Nostrand Avenue, Black solidarity rang out. Due to the 'brazen' acts of the Black Panther Party, a political organization founded on the West Coast, Oakland on Berkley's Campus and headed by Bobby Seal and Huey P. Newton, Black pride was ringing out loud. Scared, the government got involved by exerting overt racial oppression, using the NYPD as a defense. Founded on the ideology of Black nationalism and socialism the Panthers sent J. Edgar Hoover into a tizzy. Like Malcolm X, the Black Panther Party for Self-defense believed that peaceful disobedience was nothing but a whitewashed attempt to pacify White folks and would do nothing to liberate Black folks. Armed and ready the Panthers were proving to be an effective and influential organization. With their Ten-Point Program, which included an immediate end to police brutality in our neighborhoods, they were succeeding in showing the independence of Blacks from White America. Hoover's counterintelligence organization, the FBI, considered the Panther Party the greatest threat to national security and made them a target of COINTELPRO—a secret arm of the FBI. Due to the 'brazen' acts of the Black Panther Party, the response was to flood underserved neighborhoods with neutralizing and debilitating substances…drugs, and to up the ante on police brutality. But Black folks were ready. The Race War of 1968 came on the heels of growing Black pride.

Out of busted windows and jacked-up doors of decaying homestead flowed protest music. Marvin Gaye's, *What's Going On*, Harold Melvin and the Blue Notes, *Wake Up Everybody*, Miriam Makeba's, *Young Gifted and Black* and of course James Brown's, *I'm Black and I'm Proud*. Brothers rocked their afros and dashikis as did the women of the movement. I was only six at the time but life in the streets was palpable and full of hope. My older brothers were no exception. It was that year too, that during the medal service at the Olympics, two Black Athletes, Tommie Smith, and John Carlos, raised their hand in a Black Power salute during the U.S. National Anthem. Black protests had gone worldwide. They were no longer willing to be just optics of American democracy, they wanted their slice of the pie.

A leadership group called the Central Brooklyn Coordinating Committee, also known as the Central Committee, called for a truce between local rival gangs such as Sportsman, Tomahawk, and Jolly Stompers. Bishop Sonny Carson, a well-known and educated Civil Rights leader, would spearhead that movement of solidarity. He believed that the time had come for Black people to stop fighting each other and to unite for the good of all Black folks. Bed-Stuy wasn't alone; Martin Luther King Jr's assassination had put this type of sentiment into many Black communities around America and the Black Power Party added the fuel. The movement published literature on Black solidarity that one could purchase for twenty-five cents at well-known Black-owned businesses like Mr. Roosevelt's and Mr. Wilkens Candy Store.

Although I believe Mama supported the rise of the Black man, she did so in a different way. Her belief in the quote "Men should die on their feet rather than live on their knees," made me not doubt her desire to see her people on equal ground but she didn't believe everyone needed a microphone. She'd seen all too well what happened to vocal people. Mama emphasized that sometimes "nothing is the best thing to do when you don't belong." So, she would not allow any of the literature in our home. Neither would she tolerate us saying things such as, "Say It Loud, I'm Black and I'm Proud." With the mix of racial pushbacks and volatility, tensions grew and I became convinced that this was out of fear that the police would retaliate with harassment, violence, or murder. Mama's fears were justified. Vocalization of the indignities of the Black man's life story during this time only caused the local police to armor up. They were very well known for doing just that sort of thing along with destroying any literature they could get their hands on to help stop the spread of the pro-black propaganda. The Police went so far as to plant drugs on Black men and then arrest them to get them off the streets. There was no way a Black man was going to get the benefit of the doubt versus the words of a police officer in court. They were driving home a point.

Our home was just down the road from the Black Panther offices. On the street corners were also these 'cats' handing out flyers. They were fly. Always dressed in suits, they'd be promoting their Islamic faith. These brothers always seemed together and were above the fray of community fracas. Their confidence would serve to awaken my Black consciousness. When I learned they didn't eat pork I was down with that and this was my first time vocalizing my 'Black' consciousness. I promptly went home and told Mama, "I will no longer eat pork because I consider the pig as a fat, disgusting animal that has no regard for itself." What I got was a slap in the mouth. I had not known then that "pig" was an insulting slang name for the police. Besides, had I not eaten pork, I would have starved since pork, a cheaper cut of meat was what Mama cooked most days, except on special days when she would fry chicken.

The solidarity didn't last as long as the organizers had hoped. In Bed-Stuy, one must decide on *the* choice way to survive the streets. When we were younger the streets were always just outside but there were carefree times inside our home. Since Mama wouldn't let us roam the streets, we entertained ourselves by making a paper ball wrapped in tape and fashioned a wire coat hanger into a hoop to mimic playing basketball. It was during these years an unbreakable and lifelong bond was created between me and my brothers. We were inseparable doing everything together like getting haircuts, competing over the same girl, protecting each other from the gangs, and of course, playing basketball. The sound of police sirens was commonplace in the 'hood and obvious scars of a community in survival met us daily. Because of dangerous times lurking outside, Mama kept our lives safe and structured with firm discipline, school, religion, and chores to keep us busy. But living in a place like we did, trauma was inevitable, embedding itself in your soul without you even realizing it.

— TWO —

SECOND QUARTER

In the 1970s, after my oldest brother Cliff was convicted of murder, petrified, Mama struggled to maintain control of her other boys in an era where the police were no better than gangs. I never knew the full details of Cliff's conviction but when he was only in his mid-twenties Cliff had gone to a neighborhood party where an argument broke out. A ruckus happened and a local girl got in the middle of it. She was stabbed and eventually died from her wounds. Although other people were involved, Cliff was accused and convicted. He received a five-year sentence of murder in the second degree.

With Cliff away, Dale, Paul, and I became well-known as the "Scurry Brothers." Moses and Willie, who we called "Tiny," born in 1968 and 1969 respectively, were much too young for Mama to let out of her sight. A different, equally powerful bond was formed between them and Mama. Tiny even slept in Mama's room. The baby of our family, he was very much loved and adored by Mama who had more time to be with him and he was spoiled by all of us. There was no jealousy over Tiny's bond with Mama.

My sisters, the Scurry girls, were standouts. They were well-groomed, very attractive, and popular. Linda Jean, Eddie Ruth, and Carolyn (known as Gina) gave the Scurry Brothers no reason to have to protect them, but we did anyway. Very fiercely! Linda Jean was tall and athletic and played basketball in Junior High School 117. She was a small forward and a playmaker. Eddie Ruth had a Girl Group in high school. They sang R'n'B and gospel and she had some pipes on her. Their group was super popular in the neighborhood. Carolyn, the youngest was tall, slender, and attractive. She was studious and a real academic achiever. She was the tallest of the girls and now stands six feet tall and is still super attractive.

As we got older and grew bigger, our living quarters felt cramped. Mama decided we needed an apartment with more space. We were on the move, this time to Stuyvesant Avenue famed for Spike Lee's, *Do the Right Thing*. Transferring schools again made me sad, but I did make new friends at Public School 26 on Reid Avenue, now known as Malcolm X Boulevard. Things started out all right at the new school until I reached puberty. I hit a growth spurt and grew like a beanstalk; tall and skinny. I outgrew all of my clothes in the process and had to wear hand-me-downs that were still too small. I was teased, bullied, and ridiculed for my floodwater attire, and even chased home from school.

At Junior High School # 57, I grew even more. The bullies here took things a bit more seriously. The day after bullying us they would continue the harassment. They would laugh at us just to ruffle our feathers and get a rise which would give them yet another reason to bully us. If we didn't take the bait they would instigate fights. Amid the urban jungle, I was learning to survive. What Mama didn't understand was that every day was a war zone for those who didn't fit in. I began trying to fit in. My fitting in was a teenage rite of passage stuff like stealing candy from Mr. Wilson's store.

Mama was promptly informed that I was getting into trouble outside of school and was stealing candy from the local candy store. Even in the 'hood, it takes a village! Fearful of losing another son to the streets, Mama knew if she didn't nip this behavior in the bud, it could lead to prison. So, she implemented her own "Scared Straight Program," taking me there herself to visit my brother Cliff in the Green Haven Correctional Facility! The bus ride alone was punishment. One had to take the number 2 train to a bus to another bus and the journey was way over five hours. A maximum security prison, it housed the infamous gangsters Nicky Barnes and Ronald DeFeo whose story inspired the *Amityville Horrors* novel, about a man who killed his parents and four siblings in their home. It also had a gas chamber and a surprising number of Jewish criminals. So much so that they served Kosher food.

As we approached the visitor's reception room, the first thing I noticed was the disgusting smell of sewage. The next thing I noticed was the sloppy-looking guards—all of them were White and most were wearing shirts stained with chewing tobacco. Many were also very obese. It was good to see Cliff. Though he looked physically the same I could tell his spirit was broken. I talked with my brother for a long time.

"Life in prison," he said, "breaks your spirit, destroys your state of mind. It crushes your hopes and dreams until you become institutionalized. All I hope for when I wake up each morning is to survive that day."

Cliff described his cell as being no more than a six by nine-foot hole with a rock-hard bed, metal toilet, and sink combo with no privacy at all to do his business. "This is now my life," he said, "twenty-three hours a day, seven days a week. We get one hour of recreation per day, which is if you want to risk your life trying to avoid being cut, stabbed, or beaten. You mind your business." Seeing my brother behind those bars and hearing his stories scared me. I never wanted to end up there. Leaving that facility made me realize one thing. I wanted a different life.

With five young men and three girls with ravenous appetites, Mama's struggle became real, real. The cost of school, doctor's bills, food, and transportation for Mama to get to and from work stretched our budget. The bills kept piling up beyond Mama's means. Mama was doing all she could to put food on the table and to keep a roof over our heads, even in the most run-down of places. We had no choice but to move yet again. Mama found us a place closer to her work in Williamsburg, Brooklyn.

Williamsburg bordered Bed-Stuy but you might as well be on Mars…they were so different. On one hand, it certainly didn't help that the school and neighborhood were predominately Hasidic Jewish and Hispanic as we stuck out like huge sore thumbs, but on the other, it was a lot less chaotic and safer than Bed-Stuy. Our new home was also closer to our family physician, Doctor Rabinowitz, on South Fourth Street. He was within walking distance from where we moved on South First Street. I was now twelve, 5'8", and transferring to yet another school, Junior High School 50. The constant transfer was wearing on my academic grades as I couldn't stay focused on anything. I wasn't a good student to begin with and I had a hard time keeping up.

The new neighborhood was indeed safer and had government programs to help families with things like child nutrition, offering school breakfast and lunch, medical needs, employment, and housing. Face-to-face was one of those government programs that helped Mama. We could not have survived without it. Before Mama could qualify for this program, all of us kids needed to complete physicals including getting shots. Mama would take Caroline, Moses, and Tiny. Dale, Paul, and I would walk to the Doctor's office together because we were old enough. Getting the shots wasn't that bad even though they did hurt. The worst part was being thirteen and at the beginning of puberty because the physical exam was very embarrassing, especially when the doctor held my manhood and told me to cough.

It was now the mid-1970s and life for Black people was seemingly starting to get a bit better and slightly easier, for whom I do not know, but that was the talk. As far as I could tell, the Black neighborhoods were still plagued by inequality and neglect. Williamsburg offered us some carefree times we didn't have in the old neighborhoods.

The walk home with my brothers from school or the doctor was like an adventure for the four of us. We raced and played throughout the neighborhood just like normal kids. We felt happy and free. In time, Mama felt secure enough to set an 8:00 p.m. curfew on school days and a bit later at 9:00 p.m. on weekends. Being able to explore the neighborhood helped us fit in and make new friends. Paul, Dale, and I always stayed together. Where one went, we all went. We were the Scurry Brothers!

On one of our journeys, we found the local swimming pool on Metropolitan and Grand Avenues. It was great and we spent many hours there. Sometimes we would walk over to McCarren Park on the north side, which was mostly Italian and Polish. After our day's activities, we would go to our favorite pie factories. Because we were so poor, at home food was rationed. The gnawing hunger in our bellies from barely enough food to go around made us feel like every day was a struggle. But our answer for a belly full came from day-old pies specifically set aside from the new batch that we would get for cheap. There were Hostess, Drake's, Sara Lee, and Entenmanns. All the pastries were delicious and filled our stomachs. The trauma of poverty and lack was settling in my bones.

Heading back to the south side, we'd pick up our local stray dog, Blackie, to accompany us and our homemade go-carts as we made the rounds. We would race our carts down Wythe Avenue and Grand Street to the East River. The last one there would have to run home and steal milk from Mama's fridge to wash down the day-old pies. The rest of us would hang back outside and observe with envy the older guys, who were addicts but played great basketball in the park behind Public School # 84 on Wythe Avenue.

For some reason, most of these guys had pigeon coops on their roofs. Was it a status thing or an expression of how cooped up we were as Black folks? I often wondered. One of the guys, Sonny, had one of the biggest coops in the neighborhood. Mama said I could have one if I took care of it. After gathering up old pieces of wood from around the 'hood and making my coop, I went out and got some pigeons. I had Flying Flights, Tiplets, and American Flying Tumblers. It's a New York City thing. In places like Manhattan, pigeons roamed free. Our pigeons lived their entire lives trapped in elaborate coops perched on top apartment rooftops. Their lives depended on being cared for by their owners. My pigeons gave me a sense of great pride. My coop was located on our roof where I could look over the edge of the roof and see the social club in front of our house. I would watch B-Boys dancers, break-dancing, and the doo-whoppers—the old timers getting down and harmonizing to the oldies but goodies songs. It was my private world where I could dream. I don't remember exactly what I dreamed about but I knew it had something to do with a better life.

That summer I joined the Young South Side Brothers Dance Club. Initiation to get into the 'gang' involved fighting one-on-one and two-on-one with our opponents. It was hand-to-hand fighting and we had to show that you wouldn't back down no matter how much you got beaten up. It was a hoot as all the members of the club were Puerto Ricans except me. I was Black and the tallest and strongest member, so I became their strong arm. Whenever there was an altercation with other social clubs, they would call me to scare the rivals and show force. Many of these rivals were scared of me because of my size since most of them were also Puerto Ricans, and smaller in stature. I don't think we did a whole lot of dancing in that club but we kicked back and had fun.

Then our social clubs became something more like "gangs" rivaling other neighborhood gangs. As far as gangs go, we were benign. We committed petty crimes and stole things. We'd also ride our Chopper and Apollo bicycles around our neighborhood whooping it up. People would be terrified seeing a gang of fifteen 'hoodlums' riding together. We graduated to selling marijuana out of a brown bag but were forbidden to use the drug, one, so we would stay vigilant and conduct our business professionally and two, we wouldn't smoke up all the merchandise and therefore the profits. A few of the guys in the gang got caught sniffing glue and they got kicked out of for good.

Our social dance club would eventually organize to become a true criminal gang with the leaders carrying guns and selling real drugs. One of the hardcore guys was an ex-Marine I idolized. His name was Ziggy. Ziggy had holsters that held guns and other military equipment. He was tall and I was growing rapidly, so he became a role model for me. Ziggy was really smart and strategic. He responded quickly and effectively to challenging situations. Man, that cat, under different circumstances could have been on Wall Street. His whole way of life however made you want to get out of the gang altogether. I looked up to him but I didn't want to be him. Venturing out on my own from time to time, another role model I admired was another of the gang leaders, Benny. Benny was the toughest dude in the 'hood and he commanded respect from everyone. I looked up to these guys and though hustling was not my thing, my attitude toward the streets changed.

Unfortunately, in 1977, when I was fifteen, I joined a gang. It was a frighteningly bad year for the Scurry family. Upholding the code of honor of the older gangsters, I hid being a gang member from my family. I never discussed things with my family about the drugs they were bringing into the neighborhoods. As drug use skyrocketed in the '90s, the very fabric of our community, culture, and lives were being snuffed out and overrun. A new type of gang had emerged. The new gangs had no code of honor and even the Young South Side Brothers broke up because these cats were hardcore. Heroin and those who sold it were fast becoming the kings of the streets. Little did anyone realize that this was organized and intentional destruction, a new tactic to subdue Black folks. All the pusher men and boys saw was the paper that gave them bragging economic rights. No one was laying low. They were all about the bling. People's Park in Williamsburg was a safe place to go after school to have fun until dead bodies started showing up. The park became littered with drug paraphernalia, empty dope bags, and used syringes. Friends who were good people became junkies overnight.

One evening my brother, Paul, had a dispute with a well-known gangster over something I never knew what. Paul got the better of him, knocking him down hard. When the gangster got up, he pulled a gun and shots rang out. Paul lay on the ground in a pool of blood from a shot to the back. I stood by in shock. The gangster pointed the gun directly at my face. It scared the shit out of me, but he did not shoot because all hell broke loose as neighbors flooded out of their apartments. With too many witnesses, he fled like a bolt of lightning. I was scared out of my mind. If ever there was a warning that I needed a different life, this was it.

Our fate would be tested during the court proceeding. Our family members were being harassed and threatened by the gangster's associates. Out of care and concern for her family, Mama decided we needed to move, again. Before moving though, I decided I had to get revenge for my brother. I borrowed a 22-caliber pistol from one of my friends, found the gangster who'd shot Paul, and chased him to his home. I would have shot him dead were it not for Mama.

Somehow, she got word that I had a gun and tracked me down before she lost a third son to the streets. Mama smacked me hard across my face, took the gun out of my hand, and ordered me home.

Paul was the final test for Mama. She was not going to let the rest of her sons go down that same path as the hoodlums of the streets. Mama sternly reminded all of us of the day the detectives came to our house to tell us that Cliff had committed murder and that it would be best if Mama talked to him, to help convince him to turn himself in. I didn't need much reminding about that time as I remembered it vividly. When the detectives left there was a trail of white cigar smoke that followed them. I will never forget the 90th Precinct and how blatantly they disregarded police policy trying to be judge and jury without due process. When the court proceedings began, Mama had no money for a trusted lawyer, much less a lawyer period. So, the court used Paul as an example to the neighborhood. I mean he was the one who was shot! I was furious and now fully aware of the inequities of Black life in the 'hood, if not in all of America. At some point when living in the margins, you make a decision. Cower or fight.

Paul did not go to jail but the bullet that traveled through his body changed him. He survived, but he was never the same. We moved again. 340 Clifton Place in Bed-Stuy became our new home. We did not know anybody in that particular part of the city and it was a whole new environment.

While Cliff was locked up in Greenhaven, and Paul incapacitated and recovering, Bed-Stuy descended into the abyss. Warring over who would become the next super gangster such as Bumpy Johnson, Nick Barnes, or Fred Myers cost the 'hood many lives. Bed-Stuy was becoming desensitized to the daily violence and murders, which had become the norm. Hearing gunfire at all hours of the day and night, very young kids were familiar with the sounds of gunfire and were taught how to run for cover. Living in Bed-Stuy compared to the bordering Williamsburg, was as if Williamsburg wasn't even on the same map.

This Bed-Stuy was a 'hood pockmarked by numerous low-income housing projects called L.G., Tompkins, Marcy, Brevoort, Louis Armstrong, Roosevelt, Farragut, Fort Green, Red Hook, and Gowanus. They housed thousands of oppressed Black families seeking equality by any means and were breeding grounds for criminal activities and hard-core criminals. Mama, hearing about the gang violence coming from these projects forbade us from venturing down Nostrand Avenue, the heart of the projects. She understood all too well the dangers for boys of our age and color. Meanwhile, gangsters like Monster Steve, T-Rock, Homicide, Puerto Rican Supreme, and Kelvin "50 Cent" Martin were doing everything they could to destroy and control the projects with drugs and murder. Others were doing their best to save the 'hood. People like Hank Carter, Richard Green, Sonny Carson, Imam Siraj, and others set up community centers and hosted respectable block parties where even the neighborhood junkies could safely participate in the festivities. The red Johnny pumps (fire hydrants) were all illegally opened and water flowed down the street at full blast. Koolman Ice Cream set up their truck and gave free ice cream. DJs set up their equipment tapping into the streetlamps for electricity before the cops arrived to shut them down. The neighborhood was finally experiencing some normalcy for the betterment of these good, law-abiding Black folks. Or so we thought before mayhem broke loose.

Paul and Dale were eager to assert their presence throughout Bed-Stuy, aiming to become the Kings of the City. While I had spent most of my life in the quieter neighborhood of Williamsburg, I understood the allure of the streets, where everyone harbored dreams of dominance. Bed-Stuy had evolved, relinquishing much of its past for the allure of wealth, drugs, crime, guns, and gang activity. Paul and Dale's dominance was around basketball not drugs. If Dale had gotten a whiff of my activity selling weed, he'd have knocked me upside the head hard. I probably would have been TKO'ed. Completely knocked out!

— THREE —
RACIAL CONSCIOUSNESS

It was now the Reagan Era and the war on the very drugs they used to infiltrate and ghettoize Black neighborhoods had crossed over into lovely middle-class White neighborhoods. White kids were becoming junkies and would come to cop drugs in the neighborhoods. Unfortunately, the NYPD thought a war on drugs meant "A War on Black Men." Racial profiling meant only one thing. If you were a Black male, you were guilty. The already volatile relationship between the cops and the community was at an all-time high. If they couldn't find drugs and/or weapons on you, they would plant them on you and cart you off to the pen. Of course, in court, a Black man was always guilty. I'd seen this happen far too many times and the more it happened the more hopeless we all felt. This period also saw the rise of the Prison Industrial Complex where rich folks could get richer lowering the cost of labor by using prisoners to fill jobs. Today private prisons generate 4 billion in profit for those with a vested interest in its expansion. Just look at the number of Black American lives that have been needlessly taken by the hands of trigger-happy cops showcasing the racism so deeply buried in the marrow of American society. Life was sending mixed messages then as it is now.

Though we'd moved back to Bed Stuy, I continued attending Junior High School #50 in Williamsburg but my grades continued to go down. I had no support or academic help as the educational assistance programs were being cut. As my grades suffered I began losing even more interest in school. Idle minds, as they say, are the devil's workshop. I started playing hooky from school. For fun, I would ride on the back of public buses, as a sport, a dangerous activity, and very foolish. I was also jumping subway turnstiles which of course is illegal. I was becoming a small menace to society. Most of the time though, I hung out at Rafaelito Irrizary's who lived on the same block. Going to his house was a welcome escape as it was a completely different culture than mine. Rafaelito had what I called the luxury of freedom. He never had to tell his parents where he was going and had no curfew. When I was there, he would make ice cream shakes and we could raid the 'fridge as it, too, was not off-limits as it was in my house. I envied Rafaelito and his Spanish heritage with its colorful festivals and abundant food. I savored the traditional *pasteles* and beans and rice dishes. Rafaelito had a world unto himself, and I wanted my own. After years of just listening to Mama, I was going to start thinking for myself more seriously. Sometimes when playing hooky, I would go to the A&P supermarket to pack and deliver grocery bags for pocket change. At fifteen, sporting some chin fuzz made me feel grown up. Spanish workers in the supermarket utilized my speed and strength to run up and down the stairs of tenement buildings to deliver the heaviest grocery bags so they could deliver the lightest bags. I could make fifty deliveries in a day and end up with a very welcome pocket full of change.

1979 was my final year in JHS 50 and I was still struggling with my grades. My brother Dale had moved on to the Boys High School a few years back and talked a lot about the fun he was having playing basketball. But my grades were only good enough for entrance to Automotive High School, a local trade school on the north side of Williamsburg. They did not have much of a basketball program. Paul, thank goodness made a full recovery from the gunshot wound and he, like Dale, loved basketball. They, as I said, wanted to be dominant players in the community. By then, I had outgrown all my brothers. I was now 6'4" and weighed 180 pounds. While attending Automotive High School because of my poor grades, I also had to attend summer school. But during my free time, my older brother Dale would teach Paul and me what he learned from his coach, Frank Mickens at the Boys High. We were good and at my height, I was a natural.

In time, our basketball moves improved and we practiced our new skills against some local legends in the park at Public School 84. To improve our game, when we got home Dale being the oldest, had control of our little black and white T.V. and he'd insist we watch the Philly 76ers and the Boston Celtics playoffs. Dale wanted us to study Dr. J and try to copy what he did, hoping we wouldn't get beat as badly when we went up against some pretty well-known players. Dr. J or Julias Erving II was a New Yorker and he was the badass who invented the slam dunk. Erving won three championships and four MVPs and played for the 76ers.

Though I played alongside my brothers, I wasn't all that interested in ball and would skip out on playing. Once during a game, Dale was short a player and because of my height, he wanted me to fill in. That's all it took for me to catch basketball fever. I would zig-zag across the court dribbling and scoring. I was so up in these moments of triumph that every worry I had seemed out of sight and out of mind. Anxiety was replaced with a rush of excitement.

I started playing for real. After winning a few games, we were once again known as "The Scurry Brothers." It was then that I knew passion and it was an alternative because I didn't want to get along by going along with the streets. I was born a stallion, that much I knew even if I hadn't yet fully realized it. What I did know was I was geared up to run this race of life and despite the circumstances that aimed to clip my wings and render me another statistic, I was going to jump hoops and head to the finish line.

Our game became legendary. When new families moved into the neighborhood, they would hear about us and would challenge us. It became brothers against brothers, cousins against cousins and it was very competitive, yet extremely fun. Dale and Paul had experienced this feeling of freedom having played organized ball. Dale, getting lessons from Coach Mickens was a real student of the game and had honed his skills playing with the older ballers who though many were addicts, were still great. If you didn't know them personally, you could not tell that they were addicted to all sorts of drugs. Paul went on to play for the L.I.U. Blackbirds.

Now, I had the same feeling of control. This freedom to control something because I could was heady. Yogi, a Spanish neighbor, comes to mind when I think of support for our talent in Brooklyn. He saw our flair and guided us to sharpen our game to a whole new level. Yogi even put the word out on the streets that we were the team to beat. He encouraged me to get into a school that had a sponsored basketball program because I had what it took to go pro. That was far from my mind, but I was a natural.

While we continued to develop our game, Mama found all kinds of ways to pay our bills to help buy our basic necessities. Without any help from our father since he'd stopped coming around altogether, I wanted to do what I could to help. To help Mama, I would bet my friends that I could jump over the hood of their cars. I would fly through the air like a feather and always clear my mark. I would race against older players, leaving them in the dust. My sister, Eddie Ruth, stopped by one day to watch us play against another neighborhood team that had sought us out because of our local fame. She was so inspired by how well we played that she set up a game with a group of old-time gangsters in the Bed-Stuy. These guys had ballers, some even better than NBA players and they played for real money. They went by names like Dancing Harry, Shug, Sheriff, Microwave, Secret Weapon, and Beetle. For as great players as they were individually, they were not as organized as we were. Basketball is a team sport and their lack of collaboration skills kept them from playing team ball, so "The Scurry Brothers" won games by a few points and were a few dollars better off each time. Our popularity grew and recognition grew in the mean streets of Bed-Stuy—the Mecca of Basketball. With Dale standing at 6'5 and Paul at 6'3, they were on the smaller side of players. But even with taller point guards and centers dominating the court, they excelled. As for me, standing at 6'8", I had real promise.

We might have been stars on the court but off the court, with six other siblings, we continued to share our only bathroom in our cramped quarters. Mama, making the most of our humble surroundings with resilience and love never failed us. The Scurry's, despite it all, soldiered on.

Bed-Stuy turned out to be the answer to Mama's divine prayers and a blessing for all her kids. Because of our reputation on the courts, we were welcomed with open arms. That meant we would be revered and out of harm's way. Relief finally replaced the lines of worry constantly etched on Mama's face when she saw how the 'hood embraced her boys. Basketball, if not my calling, was my superpower. In my third year at Automotive High, my oldest sister Linda saw how I was struggling with my grades. She also saw how good I was on the courts. Linda talked to Mama while Dale talked to Coach Mickens about allowing me to transfer to Boys

High under his watch. Mickens considered me an underplayer with no chance to go pro. In his mind, I was just a skinny kid learning the game who had a knack but no future in the sport. He passed me down to Coach Ray Haskins at Alexander Hamilton High as a second-rate player. Mama had her concerns about me going so far away, deep into Brooklyn to school. Her fears were justified because all the danger she had heard about in that area was evident. My sister Linda reassured me, that she would support me with whatever I needed as long as I gave my best effort. With three-and-a-half years of eligibility remaining and having spent only a year in Stuyvesant, I still hadn't fully acclimated to the neighborhood vibe. I however was determined to buckle down.

Coach Haskins persuaded Mama that I would be ok, stating he would invest time with me…if I were to try my best. After wasting three years at Auto Motive High School, I would have a lot of making up to do to live up to Coach's expectations. Alexander Hamilton High in Crown Heights, Brooklyn, was named after a guy named Alexander Hamilton who was chief staff aide to General George Washington. Hamilton himself hailed from some island called Nevis. He looked like a straight-up White dude but rumor had it that he could have been a mulatto—an octoroon meaning one-eight Black. He rose in his political influence to become one of the foremost authorities of the U.S. Constitution, and the founder of the nation's financial system as the first United States Secretary of the Treasury. With all that, the school was still plagued with a notorious reputation.

On Albany Avenue, across from the notoriously dangerous Albany Projects, after being told about the type of environment it was, I realized I was taking a chance with my life just by walking in the neighborhood. Robbery, stabbings, shooting, and killing were commonplace. I ditched my old sports bag and scrounged around for a bag that didn't look as feminine as the one I tooled around with. If I were going to fit in, best not be a target; I couldn't look weak or vulnerable in this 'hood. One had to adhere to the swagger of the neighborhood to be accepted—there was the walk, the talk, and most definitely the style.

The school itself looked like a basement museum of history. It was old and crumbly. Our basketball practices had to be held at Saint John's Recreational Center on Sterling & Schenectady Avenues because our gym had concrete columns that were in our way when we played ball.

On my first day at Hamilton, I was nervous and didn't know what to expect. A group of kids came over led by a short chubby dude who introduced himself as Beetle. He was with his friends, Ice, Dre, Boo, Ed, Darnel, KK, and about fifty other ballers were milling around. I felt right at home coming from a large family. Jerry "Ice" Reynolds was the star player at Alexander Hamilton.

Defense was the key to Coach Haskin's success and he was no joke. The training he put us through was something I had never experienced. In the past, it was the "The Scurry Brothers" playing but on this journey, I was on my own. The overwhelmingly competitive drill after drill, three-man weave after weave training wiped me out. After the first day's practice, I could hardly walk. My legs were sore and stiff, and I was exhausted. Completely depleted. I kept thinking about all the fundamental skills my brother, Dale, had taught me and how savvy I was at streetball, but Coach Haskins' workout was a different story. I wondered, if I'd made a good impression and if he was satisfied with his decision to take me on.

I continued to play the entire last year at Alexander Hamilton and I was ready to take my cue from some of the greatest high school players who ever lived…Isiah Thomas, Wilt Chamberlin, Alonzo Mourning. As members of the PSAL league of the Amateur Athletic Union (AAU) against the other Citywide leagues, we would go on to become the "City Champs," beating both Boys and Girls High School and some of the best AAU players in the country, Pearl Washington, Ed Pickney, Chris Mullin, and Walter Barry. We beat them all!

My team members Beetle, "Sky" Ervin, and I all lived close to each other. Cutting through the notorious Brooklyn streets with our championship jackets on, everyone knew who we were and gave us our props. Our Champion jackets were like a free pass through the 'hood and we had the protection of the local gangsters. I liked being a baller! Could this, I wondered be the beginning of my newly found dream to make it to the NBA?

One day after a grueling practice we were trekking through the projects to get to where Andre "Sky" Ervin lived on St. Marks when a known thug stopped us. That was unusual but when he singled me out and was determined to get whatever I had in my pockets, I was on high alert. Homeboy pulled out a 007 knife, threatened me with it, and chased me around a car for the measly one dollar I had in my pocket! It wasn't as though I was decked or had swag compared to the Brooklyn style of the day: a sheepskin coat, suede Pumas, and a Kangal, nor did I have the walk that says, I've got something going on. All I had was a handful of pennies, nickels, and dimes and my championship jacket. Thoughts of Paul being shot flashed in my mind. Was this also to be my fate for a dollar's worth of change? I bolted, running as fast as I could. Because I was in great athletic condition, I escaped and was even able to buy something to eat with the change in my pocket. I saved my life and I can still remember the taste of that sandwich, turkey, and cheese on a hero.

Ervin said nothing but to this very day, I believe Andre "Sky" Ervin, my teammate at Alexander Hamilton HS, had set me up. Why was the thug only interested in me? Dre, short for Andre, had been laughing and was way too calm when the incident occurred. I was the star of the team and I guessed he could have been jealous and wanted to prank me…or I hoped that this was some kind of initiation or even a cruel practical joke. But a betrayal would have been galling. From that day on I never again trusted Andre "Sky" Ervin. It could have gone wrong in so many ways.

The next day, still upset from the night before robbery attempt, I was anxious and it made practice very intense. I faltered and lost a rebound by bringing the ball down. Coach told the other twenty-two players on the team, that if I brought the ball down again they should smack my arms. Unfortunately, for more than half the practice I was getting smacked. This made me angry, and embarrassed, and I wanted to quit. Heading to the locker room, Beetle gave me one last smack. We got into a brief scuffle that almost cost us our starting positions. It turned out Coach's idea of smacking my arms was to toughen me up for our upcoming game against McKinley Tech. This game would be played at the Wachovia Spectrum, the 76ers Stadium at the time, and would be broadcast on television, Channel 2.

That day leaving St. John's, we cut through a different neighborhood where we still didn't belong. This is where I met Missy, a pretty, light-skinned girl. I liked her, but the feeling was not mutual. Our next stop was Nostrand in the direction of where I lived at 340 Clifton Place, Apt #19. It was a four-flight hike up concrete steps but since I was in good physical condition, I breezed up. On my way up, I met Doris who would become my forever sweetheart. Doris was seventeen, beautiful, compassionate, calm, about 5'6", and curvaceous. Her smile was full of pearly white teeth, framed with long straight black hair. Her brown sugar skin radiated a rich glow from her 140 pound, heart-shaped body. Doris also kept up with the latest trends in clothing, always making sure she was fly. Doris lived at the Louis Armstrong Duplex Projects, which were just a few feet from the building where I lived. I was eighteen and beginning my career in basketball. At the time I met Doris, I was 6'6" and people admired us as a couple.

Doris reminded me of Mama, centered and steadfast. Doris's dreams were like mine. Both from large families with very meager finances where there was not much to go around, we dreamed of a life outside of the 'hood. The simplest things many people took for granted, we did not have. We both had to share rooms and clothes with our siblings, and there was always a shortage of food. Neither of us ever had seconds at the dinner table. Our dream together was to have our own clothes, our home…and a more prosperous life. Doris and I would sit up late at night sharing our dreams. I would spend a few hours with Doris at her place in the coming weeks because Doris was gorgeous. But Doris had a head on her shoulders. I had Doris in my sight for sure but I was first and foremost focused on my game so our love had to wait awhile.

Fast forward to one month before the end of school and it was time for our trip out of New York City to Benjamin Franklin High School in Philadelphia, Pennsylvania. Philly, as it is called, where the founding fathers made their mark on the U.S. by drafting the Constitution, was only a couple hours away. The trip and the game were amazing. I even met my idol, Dr. J. My brothers just couldn't believe it. We brought home the win, and the news about how I played, and the prowess of our team went nationwide. Invitations began pouring in from prestigious colleges for top players. My journey had begun. I was on my way to something I could only have imagined before. I also finally had to answer one nagging question hanging over my head, "Was I doing this for everyone else or did I want to go pro?" I wanted to go pro but not necessarily for me…but for the potential of raising my family up.

Fear is like a shadow that moves with you, grows with you, and hides inside of you in the daylight. Fear feeds on the fact that the world will not support you. That you will blunder. The thing fear didn't understand was that I had my Mama's support and that was bigger than all the world. I said a silent prayer that day and said to myself, "Yes, I will do whatever it takes to play professional basketball."

Coach Haskin kept us busy over the summer by taking us to Reese Center in Queensbridge. Reese Center was run by Hank Carter who established a league of his own to help inner-city youth. By giving these kids, a safe place to go and something to do, Carter was also helping to break up the ongoing blood feuds between boroughs. Brooklyn was warring with Queens and Harlem, Bronx, Long Island, and Manhattan.

Hank Carter invented the War of Games. Not the outright war of wasted lives, but one of identifying who we were as players on the battlefield for equality. There were a bunch of kids with game or claiming to have game walking around. Hank Carter brought together all of the boroughs to unite through sports. He wanted the infighting to stop.

I traveled to Reese Center very often having to collect $1.50 carfare to get on the G train on Queens Plaza from Mama. Mama still had a hard time making ends meet. Money was always scarce in our home. Boarding the train those first few times by myself, I felt butterflies of fear in my stomach. I scanned the subway terminal looking for a face to identify with from my 'hood.

Getting off the G train and carefully walking through the maze of project buildings, I noticed a lot of rival players like Ronnie Williams, DJ Johnson, The Fleming Brothers, and Red Bruin. Entering Reese Center, the ride became a blur. I tossed off the shirt I was wearing and then started stretching out my legs and arms. I was also scanning the competition and looking to see if Dale had secretly sneaked in. He didn't want to be a distraction but rather a vision constantly supporting me. I needed a facial expression to show that

I meant business, to show my competitiveness so I traded my wide-eyed innocence for a tough no-nonsense look.

Dale's career, unfortunately, was cut short because of his school, New York Tech's small notoriety in basketball standing while Alexander Hamilton's boys' basketball was reigning supreme. By this time Dale had quit basketball to help take care of our family. Since my father was never there, he did feel the need to support us and he was next in line. He got a job at a sporting goods store to help bring in money for the family. My sister, Linda, also got a job to give Mama a helping hand and a break. My brother, Dale, became the closest thing to a father figure we ever knew. Dale was always directing us to do positive things that would make a difference in our lives.

During warmup, I learned why Reese had the nickname "The Lab." It was because it was known for manufacturing college players, high school coaches, and NBA referees. All the players at Reese were competing for scholarships to junior colleges, universities, and prep schools. For most of us, a junior college was a must before we could attend a four-year college because of 1.) our poor grades and 2.) no one could afford a four-year college unless they got a scholarship. For me, I just wanted a chance, though my grades were a serious concern.

On the first day, I played center and the competition was fierce. I did my moves, zigzagging, dunking, and taking it to the rim. I felt I did a good job. The games were fairly judged, allowing us to display our talent in its purest form. We all went home winners. I received two offers, one from Oklahoma and the other from Moberly Junior College in St. Louis. Moberley men's basketball team had a great reputation as one of the winningest programs in junior college history, with four NJCAA Championships—in 1954, 1955, 1966, and 1967, three National runners-up, and four third-place finishes. Moberly's offer was a lot better than Oklahoma but they wanted me to sign the letter of intent ASAP underscoring that if I didn't, I could blow my chances of living out my dreams. Of course, I signed, plus Moberly had long worked out its racial problems of the previously all-White team of the past and now had a solid grip on a mixed team. The truth is Moberly was hardly interested in my grades, which was just lip service, they wanted what they saw as a budding talent. I became the ultimate gym rat, training until I dropped.

— FOUR —

OPPORTUNITY KNOCKS

Always looking to firm up my identity, during my last year of high school and summer school in 1981, I joined an organization called the "Poor Righteous Teachers." Their nickname was the Local 5 Percenters and they taught what was called the 120 Degrees to many Black people who were conscious and comfortable with their culture and themselves. 120 Degrees was a booklet that promoted self-knowledge through the study of Black origins. The core belief is that the original man was the Black man and that though the social, political, and economic systems in America tried to demoralize Black folks, we were and always will be the origin of man. This group was smart and educated. They knew about people and things I'd never heard of. They knew about the Cushites of the Bible, the very word Cush meaning Black. They knew about Black men such as Russian General Alexander Pushkin, and the French writer Alexander Dumas, *The Hunchback of Notre Dame*. They knew about Beethoven, the Moor…and they knew the works of Van Sertima, *They Came Before Columbus* and *The Miseducation Of The Negro*. Being with this group was my introduction and connection to my heritage, and to my people and I made my first real spiritual connection with others who shared a common belief in our greatness. I memorized the 120 Degrees which earned me some status as a man of the people.

Black consciousness was a growing trend in the Black communities, but there were still many who displayed the traditional image of Jesus, God's son, in their homes hanging on their walls with blonde hair and blue eyes, even as they spouted *"I'm Black and I am Proud."* Talk about conditioning! I liked and took pride in the idea of our value. They switched it up for me. Without us, there was no free world. Without us, there wouldn't be much of anything.

I continued to play in local tournaments to sharpen my game. I spent hours honing my skills, perfecting my shot, and playing both defense and offense. I participated in the Lafayette Garden 270 Tournament and the Selvyn Smith Tournament, which were tryout sessions for N.A. (Nostrand Ave.) in Brooklyn. 'Rock' was our home team name. There was another great tournament, The Hole (called Soul-In-The-Hole) where games were known to produce street ball legends like Half Man-Half Amazing, Booga Smith, Willie Allen, Cliff Morgan, Bill Saddler, Fly Williams, Phil Sellers, Jerry Earl Fuller, Steve Nouns, Jeff Houston, Pete Edwards, Speedy, Dicky Lloyd, Sam Worthman, Pearl Washington, and Lloyd "Swee-Pea" Daniels. The competition was fierce, but I was determined to live out my newfound dream. My name was getting around and my game caught the attention of scouts. It was against NBA rules for scouts to approach high school or college students and they definitely couldn't approach their coach. But scouts were the people who turned dreams into reality. They found ways to make their interest known.

Before my journey to visit the campus of Moberly Junior College in St. Louis, as a Bed-Stuy kid, I had one essential stop to make. I had to play a game on the ultimate playground where every player's mettle was tested—made or broken—Holcombe Rucker Park, famously known as "The Rucker."

The Rucker was the heartbeat of Harlem's basketball scene, akin to the NBA of the ghetto and reminiscent of Ebbitt's Field for the Brooklyn Dodgers. From that hallowed Harlem court, legendary street ball players like Earl "The Goat" Manigault, Pee Wee Kirkland, Pookie Wilson, Richie Adams, Walter Berry, Cedric "Cornbread" Maxwell, and Troy Trusdale, left their indelible mark on the game. Its concrete also primed the sneakers of many NBA legends such as Wilt Chamberlain, Julius Irving, Kobe Bryant, Lebron James and Kevin Durant.

Game night at the Rucker was pure revelry. Hustlers and gamblers scurried around anxiously placing bets. People watched from perches in trees, excitement at an all-time high, knowing they were witnessing the neighborhood's main event and possibly future stars. Drug dealers who doubled as gatekeepers against interferers or bribery-tainted referees frequently offered hefty sums to sway decisions as they kept vigil ensuring the game proceeded smoothly. During my stopover, the playground, steeped in historical significance, now bore witness to the aftermath of modern-day challenges in the 'hood. The blacktop, once swept clean, now doubled as a receptacle for the paraphernalia of the previous night's clandestine activities. Still, I had to make the stop.

On that awe-inspiring day, I played with wide-eyed wonder, afraid to blink for fear of missing a play even more spectacular than the last. These players, that day, including our own Bed Stuy cohorts, defied gravity, soaring effortlessly above the rim. The Rucker was the place.

I'll never forget that day at The Rucker; Sam, also known as "The Sheriff," bestowed upon me my first taste of fame—a pass off the backboard followed by a thunderous two-handed slam dunk. From that moment on, Sam Wortham, became a mentor, and figure of admiration for me. He took me under his wing, imparting invaluable wisdom that allowed me to refine my playing style. With his guidance and the unwavering support of my brother Dale, I gained the confidence to pursue organized basketball. Sam's and my brother's support marked the beginning of my career. That day, feeling accomplished, my dreams of grandeur were ignited. As I rode the subway home, I envisioned my name emblazoned across the sky. That day I had hope in my heart. One taste of glory and my game was unlocked within the system and within my heart. The thrill of the competition and the victory that day fueled my determination and I doubled down on my efforts to become an NBA player.

Reality soon pulled me back down to earth as the conductor announced the next stop: Nostrand & Lafayette. Returning to our modest abode—a three-bedroom apartment nestled on the fourth-floor walkup of a 16-apartment tenement building—I found solace in Mama's bustling kitchen. Despite our meager means, Mama's resourcefulness knew no bounds as she whipped up meals in the same pots we once used to heat water for bathing. Right then, I wanted better for Mama. I owed Mama everything. Her nurturing presence and unwavering faith instilled in me a sense of goodness and perseverance. I will never forget her tender loving care during hard times or her forgiving Christian character that had the power to mold me for goodness even as she endured my defiance. Mama couldn't care less when being told her Blackness would hinder her progress. She never folded or cowered to anyone though she did typical Black work to support her family. Nor did she feel, or ever wanted us to feel, inferior. As Mama often said, "A free man who strives can liberate us all from ignorance."

Mama also told us thoughts of inferiority would become our prison, binding us to the limits of those who professed superiority. Yes, it was Mama's unwavering love and resilient spirit that sustained us through the toughest of times and kept that monster fear and low self-esteem in check. With her words of possibilities echoing in my mind, I envisioned a future where my brothers and I, united as "The Scurry Brothers," would overcome any obstacle in our path. The Scurry brothers were indeed poised to win. That day at Rucker's I knew, I believed, though I can't say how, that one day I would make my Mama proud and make up for all the hardships she endured because of her children.

I became serious about the game. It truly could be a way out. It could be the answer to prayers not yet prayed. It could be Mama's freedom. Learning the intricacies of every ball position began in my earlier days at Mount Carmel Catholic Church, where a gym inside the building on the north side of Williamsburg provided the perfect training ground. The Soul-In-The-Hole Tournament in Brooklyn had faded into memory, signaling the end of an era as streetball culture evolved. For me, it marked the conclusion of The Scurry Brothers chapter and the commencement of what I now term "A Hoopster's Journey." Basketball had transformed with the emergence of new-style players, marked by vicious crossovers, fancy passes, and spectacular dunks—and so had I. I adapted to new incoming styles replacing the style I had learned but had to leave behind in 1981. My adaptability was noticed. I spent hours honing my game and my style, and I became the ultimate gym rat!

My brother Dale went on to graduate from college, and was gainfully employed, but was not playing as much. I on the other hand was now setting out for Junior College, leaving behind the familiar streets of Brooklyn. I had made a name for myself and I was being noticed. I came to the attention of coaches and myriad offers came in but I lacked the D1 (DIVISION 1) grades to qualify. To qualify for an A1 college, such as Georgetown, Syracuse, Michigan, Princeton, UCONN, or Villanova, in the D1 League, I needed to have at least a B+ average to qualify. The D2 (Division 2) schools did not require grades as high and they were not as prestigious but you still had to have a passing grade. Scouts were more likely to recruit from D1 schools and that was where I aspired to be. At that time there was

"Basketball Fever" throughout the five boroughs. My idols were Dr. J and Magic Johnson. They were my role models and I felt, in my heart, that I could be the next Magic Johnson!

The AAU (Amateur Athletic Union) was where high schoolers with potential got recognized for NCAA (National Collegiate Athletic Association) inclusion at the college level. I wasn't handling my business academically but there was no doubt I was a standout on the courts. And for that reason, Moberly made me an offer. So, at seventeen years old I was setting out for Junior College, leaving the familiar streets of Brooklyn behind. Mama, unaware that the offer to Moberly was merely a tryout, bid me farewell and sent me off to a school she hoped would provide an opportunity to showcase my talent but more importantly further my education.

My first stop at Moberly Junior College in St. Louis was surreal. I was one of several recruits. As recruits, we played pick-up games to test our skill levels. I was again being noticed. But there was one other notable recruit to watch, Gerald Wilkens, brother of the great Dominique Wilkens of the Atlanta Hawks. To stay sharp and competitive, I dedicated extra hours in the gym after practice which paid off. While pondering whether the coach would build a great team around Wilkens and me, or, if my presence would cause friction with returning lettermen, I was also wondering if other recruits were promised starting spots with their signatures as well. In the business of ghetto basketball, recruiters often promised all kinds of things with no intention of ever delivering them. Sometimes it was as simple as sneakers and sometimes it was a car or money. It didn't take much for kids to sign away their talent for little or nothing. Remember approaching a college athlete is against NBA regulations, but so what?

I didn't ponder long as I soon received news of another Junior College opportunity, promising me a starting position based on my impressive performance in St. Louis. This time it was in Oklahoma. Coach Haskins my high school coach had endorsed my dedication, hard work, and my performance at Moberly which led Coach Sooner of Oklahoma to pursue me vigorously. He convinced me to sign the letter of intent and I was recruited to Northeastern Oklahoma Junior College.

Northeastern Oklahoma (N.E.O.) Junior College boasted a renowned football program, with colossal players dominating the field. I mean these guys looked like brick trucks and like they ate steak and potatoes for every meal. It seemed like an ideal setting to carve out a name for myself for their equally impressive basketball team. Unlike the intense demeanor of Coach Haskins, Coach Sooner exuded a laid-back, easygoing persona. I hastily boarded a flight home from St Louis to prepare for my next chapter. Mama didn't really understand it all. All she knew was that I was out of the mean streets of Brooklyn and that was enough.

Oklahoma presented a stark contrast to the familiar yet perilous streets of Brooklyn and it felt like stepping into foreign territory. Unlike Moberly where the population was 90.5% Black, Oklahoma was lily white. The town of Miami, OK, though small, encompassed the campus entirely, with two pubs adjacent to the courthouse and precinct. Talk about lawlessness. If you are Black in America there is no escaping knowledge of the Ku Klux Klan, the notorious white supremacist group founded in 1865 as pushback to the Emancipation Proclamation ruling. However, I was unprepared for the prevailing stories of the present-day KKK and outlaw cowboys roaming the town, their trucks adorned with rifles and Confederate flags. It was an unsettling norm that clashed with my upbringing in Brooklyn. As Mama had moved us across the country to get away from trouble, I too was cautious in this new lily-white environment and remained circumspect. There were but a handful of Black students at N.E.O.

Mr. Bill who owned the team just about owned everything else in town, from the dairy farm to the lumber yard and various other enterprises and held a revered status in town. His ostentatious displays of wealth, including massive rings adorned with diamonds, evoked images of him buying a small South American country. Though he recruited Black players, he was Oklahoman to the bone.

Everett, one of the token negroes on campus in a town of 150,000 people, and I hit it off. Everett served as a mediator for the Black students, who comprised only about 5% of the college population. We refrained from venturing too far due to lingering rumors of past lynchings. Despite segregation, the Black Student Union organization regardless of our individual geographic origin or class structure, brought us together. Fostering solidarity, support, and encouragement to excel and resist the urge to retreat home in the face of overt racism, they championed our success. We socialized with each other as the college staunchly opposed mixed-race mingling, thereby ensuring separate gatherings. Inadvertently being the trailblazers brought the younger generation of Blacks and Whites together out of curiosity.

Rumors swirled when a 6'5", 265-pound tight end from Florida was accused of assaulting a White girl, whose parents were prominent supporters of Northeastern Oklahoma's (N.E.O.) Board of Directors. Of course, being a Black man, they wanted his head hanging from a tree somewhere. The incident sparked outrage and investigations, only to reveal that it had been consensual, fueled by curiosity about the supposed prowess of Black men often exaggerated.. Fortunately, the accused player later resurfaced in the movie *Life* with Eddie Murphy and Martin Lawrence, avoiding a fate worse than death. The incident highlighted the community's aversion to interracial relationships, rooted in resentment towards a Black player who had married a Miss Oklahoma Queen years prior. Yet, I would dip my toe in the forbidden pond.

My introduction to interracial relations came unexpectedly on a hayride in Oklahoma, where I had my first real sexual encounter. Karen, yes, Karen, was a White girl and an athlete whose father was a prominent man in town. I was not even thinking about anything like sex with her but Karen was experienced. As a young man whose hormones were raging, when she came on to me on that hayride, I could not and did not want to resist. She took my virginity. We both knew the trouble that could cause when we came back to reality so we went our separate ways after that. I never hooked up with her again as I was too scared to be lynched. Yeah, you may say this was the eighties but in 1981, 19-year-old Michael Donald was lynched in Mobile, Alabama. His mother sued and got seven million dollars but that did not bring her son back and even seven million dollars couldn't entice me to bed a White girl in the open. Donald wasn't even accused of a sex crime…they just hanged him because he was Black. That's the American South for you. And it was hard going because I became the Mr. Bill of basketball. I was the team's star player and the standout guy which made me fodder for those girls who had no qualms coming on to us as basketball stars. I endured the winks and invitations and stayed clear of trouble.

— FIVE —
THE KIDNAPPING

As our team prepared for our first home game, excitement filled the air. Our undefeated preseason set high expectations and we were ready to play in front of the Mighty Norsemen's cheering fans. Our mascot and cheerleaders whipped the crowd into a frenzy and the Mighty Norsemen were unstoppable. Me and Blake "The Snake" Worthman, our 7' center were smoking. But there was nothing to do in Oklahoma! With no diversion such as girls, we would stroll the campus, looking for any excitement. We'd run into alumni playing pick-up games on a Saturday morning. The whole idea of stealing their personal goods was a dare by a fraternity member. A dare to a Brooklyn kid was a *fait accompli*. We were ready for any and everything to liven up our otherwise boring lives and environment.

So Wortman and I got up to other things than playing ball. One Saturday while the players were on the court we slipped past them into their locker room. While we were excited to finally turn up the heat on life with something adventurous albeit dangerous, we were also aware that the heist could benefit us financially. Blake served as the lookout while I meticulously scoured the entire locker room, searching every pocket for valuables. Together, we secured money, gold, silver, and studded diamond rings. Snake was tasked with holding the bag. With no time to divide the spoils, we hastily departed upon hearing the old-timers call for a timeout, indicating they were concluding their workout. Unfortunately for us, the old-timer victims were members of a fraternal organization that included judges, state troopers, and landowners simply engaging in playing ball as their routine workout.

They expected to be the sole occupants of the locker room. I guess their military instincts kicked in and suspicion arose as doors closed behind us. Observing us dart across the campus from a window only confirmed their suspicions of us as invaders of their space. As they inspected their lockers, their worst fears were realized. They had been robbed, which prompted them to summon the campus police.

Making our way hastily towards Gracy Hall, the residence of the basketball players, Blake and I attempted to maintain our composure even after sprinting a block and a half and sweating. We endeavored to blend in with the bustling crowd and proceeded to the cafeteria for breakfast. Upon receiving a detailed description of the robbery from a male alumnus, we lingered cautiously, unsure if we had been spotted and unaware of the imminent arrival of the police. The victims, members of a fraternal organization doing their routine workout, were our worst nightmare. Despite our attempts to explain ourselves as misguided youths honoring fraternity initiation, one of the victims, a prototypical redneck, Mr. Converse harbored intense animosity towards us and wanted blood. Subsequently, we were apprehended by campus police and handed over to local authorities. Surprisingly, as a Black man coming from Brooklyn, this marked my inaugural encounter with law enforcement.

The humiliation of being escorted through campus by town police officers, leading to the search of our room, was profound. I observed Blake, a towering figure from a small Arkansas town showing signs of fear unfamiliar to me. A native of Brooklyn with a more streetwise demeanor and a city dweller bound by a code of silence aka "snitching," I could tell he was so about to become a betrayer. So, eventually, I chose to confess to the authorities. My confession provided a feeling of relief, and I promptly returned the stolen items. Originally, we faced charges of third-degree burglary and possession of stolen goods. Mr. Bill the town's heavyweight and team owner stepped in. He and Coach Sooner decided that our punishment was too great. We were after all his star lineup. We were formally charged with misdemeanor theft, contingent upon the return of the stolen property. In a bid to evade harsher penalties, including incarceration, we accepted a sentence of community service and house arrest, laboring from 8:00 a.m. to 3:00 p.m. on weekdays and throughout weekends for three weeks at Mr. Bill's lumber yard. Mr. Bill's punishment, which overruled all others benefited him greatly as we were made to work over at his lumberyard toiling in the hot sun. It was like Mr. Bill's prison complex!

Our notoriety spread swiftly, making us the talk of the town. Supervised by an individual resembling Opie, we begrudgingly accepted the reality that our youthful indiscretions would haunt us indefinitely, with a permanent label as a Y.O., which stood for Youth Offender. I was not about to tell my Mama about this but as they say, nothing stays hidden forever. As our period of confinement and service drew to a close, Blake and I were forbidden from further communication, and restricted to interactions solely on the basketball court. Blake chose to leave Oklahoma upon fulfilling his contractual obligations. Following his departure from town, Kelvin Upshaw and I struck up a friendship. Kelvin was from the south side of Chicago, and I was from Bed-Stuy, do or die. We understood each other. We shared aspirations of transcending our ghetto upbringings. I was ready to put my unfortunate incident behind me and move forward with my aspirations, however, life took an unexpected turn when Rob Johnson, a dubious recruiter from Queens Bridge, resurfaced, offering me a scholarship back to Moberly Junior College in St. Louis.

When Rob and the supposed Athletic Director from Moberly, who I now suspect was a fraud approached me on Campus, he told me he'd heard of the incident I was involved with and that it could hold me back. I should start over at a place that really wanted me. Moberly. He offered to take Kelvin and me to lunch to discuss the offer I would be made. Kelvin and I hesitated. He kept insisting on me transferring to Moberly Junior College, disregarding Kelvin's objection entirely.

Leaving behind my hall of stain in Oklahoma could have been a good consideration but something just didn't sit well with me and Kelvin and I felt Rob was a rat. Call it instinct to smell a rat or honed street savvy, something was not right. Despite Johnson's assurances, Kelvin and I harbored reservations, especially since we'd learned about a scandal involving Coach Haskins. There were allegations that Coach Haskins had made under-the-table payments to lure players. Yet it was Coach Haskins who talked me up to Sooner. As I said. something didn't add up. But things would turn out quite a bit differently.

Johnson, it turned out, was nothing but a con man. He had falsely claimed to have consulted with my mother and told the powers that be that he could get me to return to Moberly. Johnson kept saying we should have lunch but I felt uneasy particularly as he forcibly guided me into the car, accompanied by the 'supposed' Athletic Director of Moberly. Strongarming me into the car, as we sped away, Kelvin rushed to alert campus police, initially believing I had been abducted as a result of a situation stemming from our jewelry heist escapade. This was the South Central after all and revenge was not unheard of.

I felt like I was in a bad heist movie. Speed bumps on the campus grounds failed to impede the reckless driving through the school zone, as onlookers sought cover. Instincts honed, my Brooklyn upbringing kicking in, adrenaline surging I entered survival mode as my mind kept ticking. What were these crazed people trying to do? This was the most bizarre thing that had ever happened to me. Memories of Uncle Andrew's teachings on self-defense flooded my mind. His guidance had kept the Scurry children safe and protected in our hood but here I was in honkey town being abducted and so I was ready to protect myself the way Uncle Andrew had taught me if I needed to.

In those tense moments, I couldn't help but wonder what value I held in Coach Sooner's eyes—whether my fate was to be dead or alive. Would the school come looking for me? Did Coach Sooner's mind race with thoughts of Carey Scurry's endangerment? Would he think Mr. Converse's relentless pursuit of revenge was the reason behind this kidnapping? If I didn't know Rob from before, I would not be hard-pressed to believe Mr. Converse was capable of this action…a racist guy through and through, he would readily lynch me.

On the journey, the two men attempted to placate me with monetary offers, coaxing me to resign from Moberly. There was promise of making a green team around me. Rob pointed out that Gerald Wilkens, whom they had made a green team around, had secured a future in the NBA. Being considered a green team candidate, meaning I'd be the player given the green light to shoot the ball whenever an opportunity arose was a big deal. It was also a big vote of confidence in my perceived prowess on the court since a green light shooter is often a team's go-to option on offense and their most trusted teammate. Unfortunately, I wasn't feeling either of them or buying into their promises, especially when I was confined to motel rooms. To avoid detection, we moved around. Days passed in uncertainty. When after days I hadn't shown back up on campus, it was decided that police intervention was necessary. With the authorities now involved, my captor's concern shifted to something far more ominous. I was scared of what would happen next.

News of my disappearance reached Mama because the school had to call her. Already burdened with the memory of past racial atrocities, she now faced the grim reality of her son's abduction. Following the news, she had a minor stroke that disabled the left side of her face, impeding her speech. She called on God's mercy. Thoughts of her baby boy dealing with the KKK or an Emmitt Till situation crossed her mind. Seeking answers she turned to Coach Ray Haskins, the man who had initially steered me toward Oklahoma. Coach Haskins, in turn, sought to reassure Mama that he was cooperating with Coach Sooner and local authorities to find me as soon as possible.

Behind the enticements of fame and glory lay a darker reality. It's not just in basketball but in many industries where fame and money are one's aim. Joe wanted to be known as a doer in the space of recruitment. Facing their psychological tactics, as the sun dipped below the horizon, the thought of leaping from a speeding car seemed more and more remote. Paralyzed by fear and hunger, the cafeteria meal of days before now a distant memory, I found myself numb and at their mercy. Arriving at another shabby Motel 6, they seemed to be deliberating their next move while keeping a watchful eye on me. Thoughts of escape flitted through my mind, but in a hostile, racially charged town like Tulsa, Oklahoma, the risks seemed insurmountable. Rob Johnson's own trepidation was palpable and his reluctance to leave the safety of the car, when we arrived at the rundown motel on the outskirts of town, mirrored my own sense of entrapment.

Somehow, I managed to convince them that they should let me call my mother. I told them that by now the school police were probably involved, which could mean they had already called my mother and the penalties for their action would be more severe. "If I called my mother and told her I left voluntarily, it would prevent a national manhunt," I said. They immediately went into action purchasing tickets for us to return to New York. At the airport, they finally complied with my wishes. With a heavy heart, I made the call to Mama from the airport, informing her of my decision to change schools, all the while grappling with the guilt of hearing her weakened voice for the first time since her stroke. It was Mama who told me to comply with their wishes. She told me to tell them she pledged to sign the letter of intent upon my return to New York if they would only return me safely. In turn, they promised a better life for Mama if she signed. They told Mama I would be home.

 I purchased new clothes and ate very well at the airport mall, compliments of my captors. The Athletic Director and Rob Johnson remained convinced that I would comply with their every demand, which I had no intention of doing. We boarded the plane bound for JFK airport under the belief that I was a Moberly Trojan. However, they made it clear that I couldn't set foot on campus without my mother's signature. The journey proceeded smoothly. We landed at JFK and left the terminal via a dark sedan that had been pre-booked for us. Every detail of the trip had been meticulously planned, with all expenses covered by these supposed representatives of the school. They called Mama to let her know we were on our way.

 I got excited as we made our way down familiar streets. As we drove down Atlantic Avenue, I remembered the Broadway Junction, a landmark for the A, L, C, J, and M trains as well as the #25 bus. The car drove straight down Fulton Street, and the journey seemed endless, block by block, light by light. Finally, we reached Marcy and Fulton from New York Avenue, and a sense of relief washed over me. I counted each block as we passed: McDonough, Macon, Halsey, Hancock, Jefferson, Putnam, Madison, Monroe, Gates, Quincy, Lexington, and Green. We nearly missed the sharp turn into Clifton Place, by Herbert Von King Park, an easily missable turn if you blinked.

It felt surreal. The oppressive thoughts that had held me captive began to dissipate. Pulling up a few feet past our tenement apartment at 340 Clifton Place, I saw a mob gathered, eagerly awaiting my safe return. As we rode past the crowd, I caught sight of Paul and his Aldo crew. I attempted to exit the still-moving car, my feet dangling out the door, but was restrained. As the mob, armed with bottles and sticks, closed in on the sedan bringing it to a crawl, my captors were scared and more interested in saving themselves and I was able to jump out of the car. I leaped into Paul's arms as soon as they tried to turn onto Nostrand Avenue. The leading detective controlling the mob intervened, preventing an attack. They hightailed it out as soon as the mob turned to welcome me home.

Rob Johnson, aka recruiter, aka con man, was a towering figure at 6'4" weighing in at over 300 pounds. He exuded an unwavering determination to claim what he felt was owed to him and had a long history of being adept at exploiting young Black athletes for his financial gain. Rob needed my talent to lure more sponsors for his sports program. Like in the streets, there is an underbelly in the world of sports. Rob Johnson was just one of the "massahs" acting as a modern-day intermediary in a system akin to slavery. Driven by greed, these exploiters manipulate young Black athletes with promises that rarely materialize. As always these usurpers built a lucrative industry off their "ghetto" talent. This enterprise of grooming young Black athletes and exploiting them for money is big business and is still prominent today. There is a whole underworld full of inner-city kids groomed by illegal betting heavyweights to engage in point shaving. The point-shaving scandals at CCNY and Boston College were both examples of match-fixing in sports.

Rob had gotten paid beforehand to "bring me in," by whom I never knew. I had no idea what happened to Rob Johnson and his accomplice after that. Their fate, along with the school's authorities involved, was to be decided by the collegiate committee's ongoing investigation. Mama's primary concern was seeing me, and her unwavering faith assured her that justice would prevail. I did hear by the wayside that Rob had been dropped from the business. I guess kidnapping was not a part of the college's coercion plan. This basketball career was turning out to be more dramatic than I had imagined.

NEW MOVES

The next step was to find a local 4-year school that would accept me despite my failing grades. By then, Paul had resumed his studies at Rockland County Junior College and was playing for L.I.U. (Long Island University). He still had two years left on his scholarship with the L.I.U. Blackbirds. Affirmative Action and similar programs aimed at uplifting those at the bottom of the socioeconomic ladder were in vogue. I was going to L.I.U. As friends, neighbors, and church acquaintances shared their thoughts and encouraged me, I began to grasp the full potential basketball held for me. There had to be something to this if I was kidnapped for it. I was, in their eyes, a prized horse. In mine, it was like a ticket out of the poverty and oppression that had plagued my ancestors and a way to honor my God-given talent. After all, who looks a gift horse in the mouth? One should show gratitude for that which is given. I thanked the Almighty.

I began wearing my hair in a low-cut Caesar style brushed to the side. After enduring my ordeal, which meant I had promise, I suppose, many schools offered opportunities that any city kid would typically jump at. LSU, Bonaventure, St. John's, N.C. State, University of Las Vegas, and The Aggies (San Diego State) were among them. I turned them all down except for L.I.U. as Mama insisted I had to be near her.

At L.I.U. Coach Wachtel delivered a speech praising my potential, reminiscing about my days as a public school player and how

I had progressed over the years. He expressed his desire to coach me in the near future. While others showered me with compliments, it was his assurance that I would start immediately that truly caught my attention. The old Paramount Theatre stood across from Juniors, the renowned cheesecake restaurant. Memories of my performances there in the Summer Leagues in Brooklyn resurfaced as I was introduced as the next Blackbird. The crowd erupted with excitement, their cheers reverberating all the way from the small gym all along Jay Street. Finally returning home after other players had departed for larger schools gave me the opportunity of a lifetime. I guess I'm a Brooklynite through and through.

As I looked around, I noticed some of the most somber faces I had ever seen from the surrounding projects—Lafayette Gardens, Fort Greene, Farragut, Gowanus, Brevort, and Marcy as teammates. Despite any doubts, the coach's pitch had convinced me. I was set to become the campus's new star, especially since they were losing Riley Clarida to the NBA Draft that year. So, I enrolled at Long Island University. Attending a smaller school, with my brothers and family nearby, felt like a blessing after the ordeal in Oklahoma.

Keeping a low profile, I dedicated myself to practice, often staying late to explore the nuances of D1 basketball and to visualize my opponents' defensive strategies. I even deliberately made mistakes during these sessions to simulate real-game scenarios. Initially, I sat out the first half of the season to accumulate enough credits to be eligible to play. I would go to observe from the sidelines as young Marcus Gaither, a potential Hall of Famer in the making, led the Blackbirds to a defeat against Fairleigh Dickinson University. Before these boys, the gymnasium, seating only 1,500, had maybe 1,000 spectators.

Occasionally, I attended home games to observe the team's performance under coach Lizzo's guidance. Despite his best efforts, it was evident that he wasn't cut out for the D1 level and was perhaps better suited for high school coaching.

HALFTIME

(left) Carey Scurry, 1st team picture from LIU (Long Island University), 1983
(center) Brother Tiny (Willie), sister Gina, brother Moses, c 1971
(right) Mama, Mildred Jones Scurry, c 1970

(right) Doris Dickerson and Carey's son, Khaleef, c 1988
(left) 340 Clifton Place, Brooklyn, NY – Family apartment growing up, c 1960s

Carey Scurry

Carey Scurry (center) Brooklyn, NY
Soul in the Hole Summer
Tournament, 1981

Carey, a sharp dresser, North Eastern
Jr. College, 1981-1982

Neighborhood Teams in the Soul in the Hole Tournament, Brooklyn, NY, c 1981

Promo - BasketBallHeadzz, Celebrating NYC Basket Ball History, YouTube Channel, 2023

New York Daily News
Spotlight on Great People
article by Clem
Richardson, c 2000

Utah Jazz Team Picture, 1985-86. Carey, small forward
(bottom row, 2nd from the left)

Carey Scurry's # 22 Jerseys

Utah Jazz Team Photo,
1985-86 Carey, small forward,
2nd from left, bottom row

A Hoopster's Journey

CEDAR CITY — Jazz forward Carey Scurry comes back down to earth after one of his many slam dunks. Martin Nessley could only look and watch. The Jazz cruised to an easy victory against the Los Angeles Clippers in their first exhibition game of the season. (Spectrum / Kris Loosley)

Cedar City, Utah - Jazz Forward, Carey Scurry executes a classic alley-oop play against the LA Clippers.

Utah Jazz poster of #22 Carey Scurry with #41 Thurl "Big T" Bailey

Curry Signature Flight Move

Utah Jazz #22 Carey Scurry playing against Boston Celtics players #20 Darren Daye and #50 Greg Kite, c 1987-88

#22 Carey Scurry Single Shot photo and autograph from the Utah Jazz

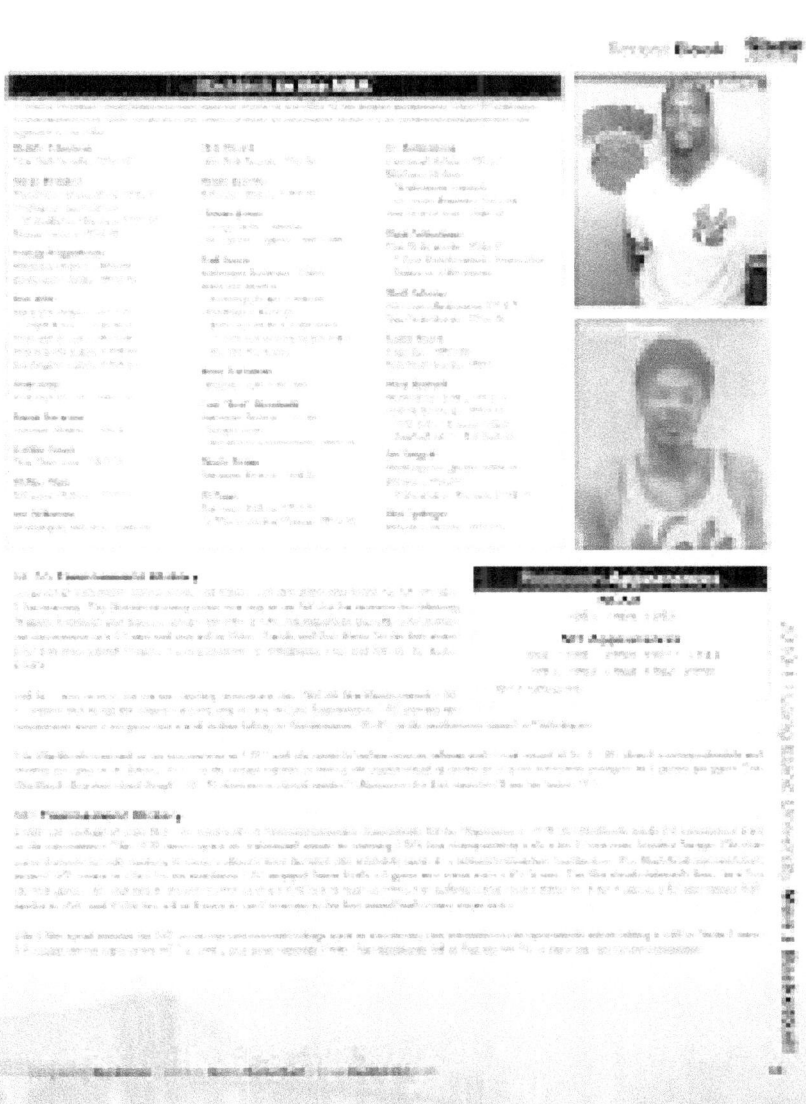

Successful LIU players' list making the NBA

Carey's #20 Jerseys from the NY Knicks

#10 Carey Scurry, small forward, with the Greek team, Olympiacos B.C., 1989-90, (left) #6 Angelou Vangelis (right) unidentified

(Left) #7 Carey Scurry, small forward, Spanish team Grupo IFA, 1994
(Right) #10 Carey Scurry, small forward, with the Greek team, Olympiacos B.C., 1989-90

#15 Carey Scurry, small forward for the Club Ferro Carril Oeste Basquet, Buenos Aires, Argentina drives past Carl Amos, GEPU San Luis, Argentina.

#10 Carey Scurry, small forward, with the Greek team, Olympiacos B.C., 1989-90

Carey Scurry, small forward, for the Rapid City Thrillers, Radpid, City South Dakota, c 1989-90

#23 Carey Scurry, small forward, played with Colo-Colo
(officially Club Social Deportivo Colo-Colo), Santigo, Chile, 1990-91

Clipping from Santigo, *El Diario*, Chilean newspaper

#15 Carey Scurry, small forward for the Club Ferro Carril Oeste Basquet, Buenos Aires, Liga National de Básquetbol de Chile (LBN Chile), c. 1993-94

Carey on "Just Gimme the Mic," radio internet and TV show" hosted by CoCo, c. 2005

Carey wearing a sweatshirt and hat from his nonprofit,
A Hoopster's Journey Prospect Park, Brooklyn, NY, 2017

Carey coaching neighborhood female players at New Heights Youth Gym in
Brooklyn, NY for his nonprofit, A Hoopster's Journey, 2023

(left) Shake-A-Vel (@shakeavel) from Drilann Entertainment with Carey at 305 Park School in Brooklyn, NY, 2023.
(right)Carey making a personal appearance with basketball players from PS 256 Brooklyn, Zone 6 Park, 2023.
Carey coaching neighborhood players through his nonprofit, A Hoopster's Journey

— SIX —

THIRD QUARTER

Walking to L.I.U. from our family home at 340 Clifton Place, I passed through the notorious Fort Greene Projects—a 15-block trek. These projects were home to L.I.U's die-hard fans. The environment alone was a threat to my career as it was no stranger to violence and mishaps. Before the renovation, the L.I.U. arena was the old Paramount Theatre on Ashland Avenue, facing Brooklyn Hospital. Sirens and police lights were common sights on weekends due to violence on nearby Myrtle Avenue. I spent considerable time pondering whether I would ever reach the point of playing D1 ball, especially after encountering trouble in Oklahoma.

But now, everything was falling into place. As word spread about the new talent in town, I began to stand out in elite circles. I became the team's franchise player with promises of a starting position. This was a big responsibility because as a franchise player, I was considered the foundation of the team and my presence would greatly influence the team's success and reputation. I was an L.I.U. Blackbird. In 1935, L.I.U. changed the color of the team uniform from blue to black. As the story goes, a *Brooklyn Eagle* reporter from the Midwest was watching the team dribbling up and down the court and commenting that they looked like Blackbirds. The name stuck and the new nickname and the mascot became a Blackbird.

L.I.U. was a great move for my career, however, we were not considered on par with schools like Marist, Fairleigh Dickerson, St. Francis, Wagner, and Robert Morris due to the caliber of players we had. This created feelings among seniors that their futures were being overlooked. The one thing L.I.U. had that made it notable was local celebrities like Chris Rock and Spike Lee in attendance at games. My career and the crowd grew overnight. Initially, attendance at the arena was under 1,000. We went from fewer than 1,000 at games to over 1,500 attendees plus with standing room only. Public attention and celebrity status put L.I.U. on the map, making it akin to a miniature Madison Square Garden. I was killin' it. Finally, I came to believe I was special, just as Grandma Ruth used to say. Reputation-wise I was a star player and I had legitimate fans cheering me on.

Despite my newfound success, poverty remained a challenge. Every meal counted as I needed to be in optimum shape. I relied on favors from teammate Ty Whitehead's sister who worked at a nearby Kentucky Fried Chicken. Ty would get in line while I hung back and his sister would give him a full bucket of chicken for a reduced price or sometimes free. My lack of trendy clothes was a social barrier to my rising stardom, so I improvised by sewing Lacoste, Polo, and other logos onto plain shirts so I could fit in. Women and basketball go together like hand in glove. It was about then that I met a girl named Delores "Sweetie Girl" Wilson from the Fort Greene Projects. She had a crazy body, was stylish, and was drawn to me because of my on-and-off-court reputation. She was very popular on campus and ran with a group of pretty girls always around her who attracted eyes wherever they went.

Back in my 'hood, I had long left behind my hayride romp. Doris and I were an item. Encountering numerous opportunities at fraternity and sorority parties, I fully indulged in the social scene and was always having sex. I moved into the campus dormitory, my brother Paul's room adjacent to mine. My room, 15J, became the VIP section for his parties in room 15K. I decorated my pad with a red light, a designer curtain I got from Mama's old closet, and other things I obtained from local 'hood boosters. We were party central. My social life flourished. Unbeknownst to me while I was stepping to Delores and others, my main squeeze and forever sweetheart Doris was pregnant. Usually while walking the 15-long blocks from L.I.U. to my home, I would sneak over to her house to check on her, get a home-cooked meal, and relax with her. By this time, we were heavily sexually active, another of my fear escape tactics. Doris became pregnant in my sophomore year. She was told to have an abortion.

Like my prowess on the court, word got around about Party Central…my dorm room as the happening place. Mrs. Gail Haines, the school's provost, intervened upon hearing about my behavior. I was summoned to her office.

"Carey Scurry," she began. "I see promise in you and I don't want you to fall into the same trap that many young Black men from inner cities who play basketball do. You have to reign in your partying and get serious about your grades."

Small in stature Ms. Haines had the strong punch of a Black woman and was full of motherly love. She mentored me, always emphasizing life beyond basketball and the importance of academic growth. Her guidance motivated me to improve my grades and avoid the stereotype of being a "dumb jock" who would be broke within five years like Mama would often say. I was approached as a potential player for recruitment. While I received gifts such as a carpet and a refrigerator from coaches, my brother's advice was to avoid taking money. "Don't take money, such a gift will deadlock you into future obligations."

I listened to my brother but I needed to make money somehow. Aware of my reputation as an influencer, I began selling t-shirts that read, "Black By Popular Demand" in my 'hood and around the school, promoting Black empowerment. Mama, of course, had something to say. Mama's time was the Jim Crow era so she saw things differently. Despite my mother's lack of understanding of the cultural shift, a revolution was taking place and in 1979, it was being televised in the form of the music gaining massive popularity with the birth of B.E.T. in the 1980s. Songs like the protest anthem of the sixties, *Say It Loud, I'm Black and I'm Proud* were giving way to new protest music by performers such as KRS One, Public Enemy, Africa-Lambada, Grandmaster Flash, and The Furious Five. My immersion in the cultural revolution was furthered by interactions with groups like the 5% Nation of the Gods & Earths at 44 Park on Monroe Avenue. The Hip Hop generation was born and Hip Hop music was becoming a cultural marker for young Black folks. Born of the streets, the genre lacked acceptance on Main Street and was stifled. But like everything else, Black folks just kept coming. The hypnotic beats, the potent words, and the b-boy guys in fly clothing, Hip Hop music soon crossed over into art, fashion, and dance, and was impossible to ignore. It became a cultural phenomenon. Representing freedom of speech, the music of the underserved specifically addressed the need for education and prison reform among other social issues and it resonated. Embraced by the youth of the ghetto, Hip-hop was unstoppable and was eventually embraced by the entire world. It changed an entire generation and was a unifier. Later people like Eminem, Vanilla Ice, and others were dropping beats. The entire K-pop industry of today was born on the back of

Hip-hop. Hip-hop spoke to more than Blackness, it spoke to freedom which was getting harder to come by for more than just Black folks in America. America's youth wanted their voice back.

I began to understand the power of the ghetto and at the same time, I began to realize that my education was just as important as my ball success. The coaches kept a tight leash on us regarding gaining a degree. I recall classes like Physical Education, Media Arts, and Low-level Math. I still wasn't much of a student and was never really prepared to be in an academic university setting so I struggled academically but I was able to keep playing.

We were mandated to take yearly physicals. Taking the physical felt like a cattle examination. Our teeth were checked along with our bone density. They made sure we were healthy and did everything to ensure our fitness for playing basketball. Individuality was irrelevant; they just wanted us to play. I was far from realizing then that basketball was just another chain gang for Black folks. It was seen as the path for the dumb jock who would be broke in five years after retiring. They were wrong. For many, it was an opportunity of a lifetime. There were indeed many casualties but those who survived raised the bar and changed the game and the expectations for their fellow athletes. Today almost all the Black billionaires come out of Hip-Hop or sports and entertainment. Think Jay-Z, LeBron James, Michael Jordan. Yes, the Ghetto can be as potent as it can be destructive if one is unconscious.

My eyes were beginning to open to myself. An opportunity presented itself when I was invited to speak to a group of kids at a church in Brooklyn. I felt like this would be a good chance to be a role model to my community. My talk was short and to the point. I stressed the importance of education and started to feel a sense of responsibility as great orators like Richard Green, Ed Towns, Al Vann, and Charles Barron might have felt. I came back from the event with a different outlook on life and tried getting the team together to discuss our plans as future leaders of the community. I was down with the program of Black empowerment.

    The Blackbirds were raising roofs. In our first home game, I dropped 22 points, 23 rebounds, and 7 blocks in front of the neighborhood crowd against Fairleigh Dickinson University. The crowd went wild. Yes, I was a product of Bed-Stuy, the Mecca of basketball. With the reputation of the Scurry family on my shoulders, I vaguely had Madison Square Garden in the recess of my mind's eye. I knew this was something big, whatever it was. I knew sports was a big part of the American identity, I just didn't know how much. With a "Do or Die" motto and the Stuy look on my face, every time I was on the court I was burning up and leaving skid marks on the polished floors. I was gaining top recognition and was selected as an all-American honorable mention, winning various tournaments and awards. When I walked into the gym those days there was a new pep in my step.

    Winning titles and finally living up to the hype my junior year was great. Not so much for the seniors, as their future in basketball hung in the balance. They had added pressure to adapt fast and step up their game, realizing that their chance of impressing scouts at this point in their career was slim to none. We had to remake the plays after our star player, Riley Claridge was drafted by the Utah Jazz and released to early rookie camp. The coach realized he had a 6' 8" slashing point forward type of player in me but he needed my help at the center position. I wanted to at least go as far as the Sweet Sixteen but hinged my vision on the Final Four. If I was in the lineup of the four teams that qualify for the championship round in the annual NCAA men's college basketball tournament, I had a shot at the gold ring.

    Our coaches and other players were satisfied with a just above .500 percentage win season. I wanted more. Winning the Eastern Conference Metro Area wasn't enough to get noticed as a

Division 1 school. I felt relieved that I gave 100% and set my standards high, establishing my position among my teammates. My first confrontation with Coach Lizzo was after he called me a moron for questioning our lack of high-intensity practices going into the playoffs. Looking back, I feel like L.I.U. stunted my growth somewhat as much as it allowed me to shine. If I had played for any other elite school around the state with better players, my game would have notched up and I would have not just raised the roof, I would have blown the stadium rooftop completely off the stadium.

We had an important game against a future Hall of Famer, Rik Smits, a seven-footer who could dominate a game at will. I would hear so much about this guy that I would get upset. I wondered why I couldn't get my full props. When I dropped 30 points, 26 rebounds (an L.I.U. school record), and 5 blocks plus winning against him, it finally brought attention to L.I.U. and to me. For sure there were scouts there to watch him and, for me, matching up against him was for sure a big deal. After that win, we won five straight games and after that, we were on a roll. We brought home the N.C.A.A. championship. Heading into the late '80s and early '90s, Rik and I were the new breed of players coming out of the new era of ball.

The older players were fading out. The other teams started to adjust to the new style of play, recruiting big guards who could bring the ball up the court, pushing the then 6'2" and 6'3" players into the land of giants. They started to throw offensive alley-oop plays or certain other types of plays realizing the game had outgrown them. But alley-oop, where one player passes the ball near the basket to a teammate who jumps, catches the ball in mid-air and dunks it before it touches the ground, requires teamwork, pinpoint passing, and timing. However, in the end, I had to salute the local addicts, smaller players up to my knees, and washed-up legends, OG Kenneth Ghee, balling behind the Louie Armstrong Housing Projects with a crate tied up to the fence for a basket because that was how I learned the science of the game. Old-style ball paid off for me at the college level.

Elite sports like basketball and football have a chattel mentality. The coaches didn't respect the politics of the game much less the players. They saw the cycle of abuse that the world of sports brought to players and were party to the abuse but did nothing. Out with one in with one. Back then, hordes of talent were being shifted around with no rights of their own. Getting savvy to my rights I would lay out the landscape for my younger brothers, Moses, and Willie (Tiny) who were entering high school. They were still under Mama's care and the last of the Scurry clan at home. I would come home after the season and teach them the basics to help define the dynamics of their game. My last year of college made me understand the game even more and the politics even better. I took the perspective of an analytical viewer. I would see the structure of the game and break down its defense using real-life situations. I would watch the greats and study every minute detail of how they navigated and negotiated play. I was able to see the play before it manifested itself much like I could intuit possible shoot-outs in the 'hood or other altercations. By Mama using the clock's second hand as the curfew deadline, no seconds were to be wasted.

Curfew had been installed earlier on in my years in Williamsburg. Remembering we had to beat the clock and be home at curfew on the dot to avoid one of Mama's whippings, we would become as fast as lightning. It was always a struggle against the hands of time to get what needed doing, but we always beat the clock. My clock was ticking. Time was of the essence. It was a do-or-die moment and I wanted to advance from this struggle as soon as possible. Would I get a chance, the politics of the game being what it was?

The streets don't leave you alone if you don't want to leave the streets. Getting high was a norm in the streets. I smoked weed, who didn't? The instant gratification and validation I sought as a young man was the same mindset that enabled me to indulge in drugs. The King Pin was part of an illusion of success fed to the streets and a lot of inner-city youth perceived them and themselves as the happenin' crowd…the trendsetters. "If you got, flaunt it," was the motto of the streets—the fruits of "hard" labor on display.

In reality, the King Pin was a destroyer orchestrated by the men in the House but it was easy to overlook when you could afford anything your heart desired…you had in fact attained your piece of the American pie. It was also easy to overlook the demise and havoc that peddling dope created. That was just the life of these new pusher men and women. With forever-changing facts that governed street life, long-term goals were replaced by short-term goals and instant gains were the ticket to ride. After all who knows how long one will live in the mean streets of the ghetto? This kind of thinking often allowed me to live a fast life. At first, weed was the thing that made me able to just kick back and relax in my downtime. I'd have a good sleep and be back on the job. But soon I found that during every game, I was high on weed. At the end of every game, there I was at a party. I knew this course I was taking would end positively or negatively, more likely the latter but weed or no weed, I was delivering so it was copacetic.

In the 'hood, it was the norm to boast about one's achievements. Coming from nothing without proper home training, this kind of attitude can alienate you and leave you in debt or broke when the gravy dries up. Though I knew better, I admit I was getting a bit big-headed. Walking into practice one day, my usual "I am the man" swagger evident, I noticed everybody huddled up in the corner. I thought to myself, "What's going on?" Finally, Johnny Johnson, one of the players broke the ice. "Hey homeboy," he said. "The team thinks you're getting too big-headed. Focusing too much on yourself and forgetting about the team."

They were right. I had to humble myself. Derek Powell and the others made sure I did just that. They never let up on me. The shit went on for a week. I got the message the same way Dale and Paul had taught me when I was young, playing in championship games against the Noun brothers, who were working their asses off trying to beat us.

We'd gotten a pretty big lead, then Dale called a time-out. He took me out of the game and put Jeff Butler in. There were five minutes left in the game. Jeff was getting banged around. He was fucking up everything and we went down five points. I looked at my brothers and said, "Why y'all doing this? We are trying to win," I said. "It's not always about a win," Dale said.

"Then why we playing?"

"Everybody deserves a chance. You have to develop the players around you to win. It's a must because that's what great players do. It's not all about you. It's about the team."

He was right. Basketball is a team sport and if your teammates don't trust you, you might as well not be on the team. Even after all this, I still had to learn it the hard way. But I understood how lonely it can be at the top because as the star player, a lot of people will envy you or revere you, both result in being kind of lonely. I had distractions and comfort…my girlfriends: Sweet Girl from Fort Green and Doris, my girl from Nostrand Avenue, and my feel-good drug.

My senior year was 1985. Time was down to the wire. I now made it my job to get everybody involved. Every game, I would take control of the first twelve possessions to get up 10-12 points and then turn it over to the team. I would start passing the ball around to Tye, Derek, Glen Daniels, and Stan Townes, to name a few. Coach Lizzo didn't mind my being the point center and bringing the ball up as long as I let everybody be a part of the game instead of being a show-off by scoring every time. This was teamwork and basketball is a team sport! It brought us closer as a team.

I didn't learn until my last year at L.I.U. why academics was such a challenge for me. I was still not confident about my academic development and sought help. The result, it turned out I had a learning disability. I didn't tell anybody about my learning issue. Looking back, I wondered if I really had a learning disability or if I just learned differently. So many Black boys are remediated because they don't learn the standard way. If you grow up in a household where the mug is set directly on the table…you are not going to say a cup and saucer. I who had a learning disability was able to learn Greek using an alphabet so different from my own. I was even able to pick up, though not quite as good—Spanish…. and I don't mean the Spanglish I was used to…they speak Castilian Spanish in Spain.

Reviewing my grade average, I was sure to be ineligible for anything beyond L.I.U. L. I. U. was not like primary school. Here, nobody was looking over my shoulder to make sure I did my homework. It was truly a burden keeping up with classwork and being on the road. I ended up changing my major from Business Administration to Physical Education to stay afloat. I'd given it a good run. But it wasn't enough, I thought. I resigned myself to whatever came next, but I prayed.

Facing the coach with the possibility that I wouldn't play in upcoming playoff games, was a disappointment. But to my surprise, there was a look of assurance on his face that said I would be allowed to play. Confirming my starting spot, right then and there my main goal was getting my education on track and not succumbing to a system of being a failed Black athlete, which was a dime a dozen in this community. Once my time was up, surely, if I couldn't get it together, I would be on the corner telling my story of how once upon a time, I was a great player to whoever would listen. I got so concerned about losing in the playoffs that I got high to escape the pressure. I had by now graduated from weed to coke by this time.

My family and community all had high expectations for me. I was feeling the pressure and felt my game wasn't growing to where I wanted it to be considered for going pro. The coach knew from his inner circle that the Jazz were interested in me long before, but I didn't think my skills were all that good. If I did go pro though, it wouldn't be a problem because deep inside of me I knew I could hang with the best of them. But fear is a monster that drives you in the opposite direction of your dream. It was about this time that Doris, my dream booster special girl who'd hung in with me since high school, became my number one cheerleader.

So, Doris and I ran off together…but not that far. She lived at home with her mother in Bedford-Stuyvesant and decided to come to live with me in my Long Island University dorm fifteen blocks away. Although at the time women were not allowed to share a room with a male student, I had special privileges because I was THE MAN. I was the center. Everybody looked up to me. I was MR. L.I.U. So, a blind eye was turned. One of the things about growing up in the 'hood when you get any kind of recognition, is that your ego can get oversized and delusion can set in. From my success of electrifying fans who lauded and embraced me, I truly believed I was THE MAN!

It felt like I had it all, a great game, a great girl, and a great family.

Now Doris had gotten pregnant for the second time. This time around I didn't want to feel the devastation I felt from her previous abortion. We decided to have the baby and Khaleef was born a healthy 8-pound, 8-ounce boy. We named him Khaleef because of its Arabic meaning "leader" and also 'successor,' relating it to the baby's role in continuing family traditions. Life as a young parent was difficult. After Khaleef was born, Doris moved back to her mother's home to get help with the baby. I was a father in name only as I was not actively involved in raising our child. I wanted to become the father I never had, although I was unprepared to do so and I was in the throes of deciding my future. I tried to make light of the situation, but part of me was destroyed because my conscience didn't allow me to discount the value of a life and I was, like my father, not around for Doris.

— SEVEN —
THE DRAFT

Meanwhile, my spotlight was shining bright. Frequently a new article or some news coverage would come out about me. One of the things I loved to do was to go into Mr. Wilkens's candy store on the corner of Nostrand and Lafayette Avenues and read the articles written about me. One article about me came out in the March 11th *New York Times* read of our MVP win:

> *Carey Scurry, the most valuable player of the tournament, scored 33 points, had 16 rebounds, blocked 6 shots, and made 5 assists as Long Island University defeated twice-defending champion Robert Morris, 87- 81, tonight to win the Eastern College Athletic Conference Metro tournament. The Blackbirds (20-10), runners-up to the suburban Pittsburgh team the last two seasons, earned a berth in the National Collegiate Athletic Association tournament.*

In homage, there were articles about me and my career posted prominently on the walls of neighborhood shops like George and Willie's Barbershop and Shirley's Dry Cleaners. I became a local hero and people looked up to me because I could be one of the ones who got out and could become successful. I was the one who could be held up before their children against the impossible dreams of most in the ghetto.

George, Willie, and Shirley were the forerunners of the successful Black business owners in the 'hood and it made me think about what was most important. If I failed at basketball with an education I could run a business like George, Willie, and Shirley. I had no adult male role models growing up and no male guidance other than my brothers. Mama, even being a rainmaker, couldn't possibly understand what it was to be a boy in Bed Stuy or the code of the streets, "if you have it, flaunt it." I was young, going after the big-picture dream and my arrogance superseded my intelligence. I couldn't see the inevitable, that stardom comes at a price. Even though I had failing grades, my basketball prowess had carried me through. I was becoming invincible. My education was out the window, so I withdrew completely from running around doing odd jobs to putting all of my eggs in one basket. My athleticism had a better chance than a porter's job at Albee Square Mall right around the corner from L.I.U.

I gave basketball everything I had. To help out with my kid, Coach got me a job to tide me over and it was during those two weeks in the stock room at Albee Square Mall in downtown Brooklyn, that my big break came. Back when my popularity was at an all-time high in Brooklyn, I had given my first speech at a church as a mentor for my community. A member from that church where I'd spoken remembered me and invited me to a Father's Day All-Star Game in Washington to play against the NBA finest. I was on the Eastern team with Gene Banks, Uwe Blab, Earl Cureton, and Isiah Thomas playing against the Western team which featured Magic Johnson, Dominique Wilkens, and Mark Aquirre. 6'1" Isiah, out of Chicago was one of the greatest point guards and that had led him to the Indiana Hoosiers and the NCAA championship. 6' 9" Magic, out of Michigan, regarded as *the* greatest point guard of all time, was legendary. This was my chance before the 1985 draft to prove myself. Man, I was on fire and a true team player. I was a lockdown defender and I performed well enough that the write-ups about me kept coming. Dick McQuire, the chief scout for the NY Knicks, Bill Traverse of the *Daily News*, Steve Serb of the *NY Post*, and Joe Glickman of *News Day*, all wrote about me. I was on the map. Not to talk about Magic giving me a thumbs up. The door was open and I intended to walk right through it.

Weeks before the draft, I was invited to an invitation-only basketball camp in Portsmouth, VA with Spud Webb and Charles Oakley, Chicago's pre-draft player. Here NBA scouts would rate players to determine to what round they would most likely go. Having such an outstanding game and getting a thumbs-up from Magic, made it that much easier for me to stand out. I was approached by agent Bill Pollack while another agent, Don Cronson, snooped around my dorm and home. I eventually chose Alan Herman, a sports agent who had an agency with former Knicks player Earl the Pearl Monroe who had retired in 2980 from injuries to represent me.

At the time, I didn't care too much about the '85 draft, feeling my time would come. I still felt there was more to perfect in my game. I went about my day as usual; friends calling me out from my back window to come and play a pick-up game. People in the streets were telling me to go to the '85 draft at the Garden. I didn't think I was going to get drafted but I thought what the heck and decided to go. My friend, Eric Cousar, my ride-or-die friend to this day, bought me the second suit I had ever owned in my life. The first one Mama bought for church use only. Eric Cousar's suit was by Pierre Cardin. It was beige and I looked fly. My agents Earl "The Pearl" Monroe and Alan Herman, had a limousine. It was a burgundy and black stretch limo. They sent it to pick me up. Their driver, Ron, picked me up in front of the building and people cheered me on. I had never been in a limo before and it felt magical. As I stepped into the elegant car, I felt important. It had all kinds of goodies. I'd long been smoking weed, but Ron, the limo driver, would become the plug for the exotic weed I came to know. Pulling up to the Garden and seeing legends like David Stern, Red Auerbach, and Bill Russell, made me starstruck. They were there to see the next generation of stars and I couldn't believe it, as I was really there, too.

Madison Square Garden, colloquially known as the Garden, in the heart of Manhattan, runs from 31st to 33rd Street. The multi-purpose indoor arena is home to multiple sports and entertainment events. It wasn't often that a kid from Bed-Stuy entered this world and when they do, it can be life-changing. Entering the Garden on the day of the draft picks, I was met with a frenzy and I was awed. Reporters, photographers, and dream makers milling around all added to the electric energy surging in the arena. Every big-name player was present. Spud Webb, Johnny Newman, Walter Berry, Chris Mullin, Patrick Ewing, Rik Smits (whom I had played with at L.I.U.), and Xavier McDaniel just to name a few. The '85 draft was and still is considered one of the best in NBA history. This was the first year that the new Lottery draft system was unveiled. It was a big night for all the hopefuls and it could be a game-changer.

Part of the draft's pomp and circumstance is that top names are called one by one by all teams representing their franchises. Names of players had been printed up on a hopeful team's jersey for the team that wanted them as their first-round draft pick. For Patrick Ewing, the Knicks, Washington, New Jersey, Dallas, Nets, Indiana, Philly, and Boston jerseys were made. In my book, he was the best player alive. In the arena was a sixty-six ping pong-like machine with balls floating like the lottery. This was the first year the lottery was instituted because coaches had been abusing the previous draft system of a coin flip between the worst teams in each division, some intentionally making their team the worst to gain a draft pick advantage. In this new system, for each player, a ball is released. The ball shows the winning team of the lottery who could bid for their 1st pick overall selection.

I was a bag of nerves when NBA Commissioner David Stern's booming voice announced, "The first overall pick goes to the Knicks. They have selected Patrick Ewing." The arena erupted. Ewing was hands down the best player at the time. After that, it was a long process of anticipation. What surprised me was when the N.Y. Knicks were back on the clock to pick after Pat, I swore I heard my name floating in the clouds. That cloud was the Knick fans in the upper rafters chanting Scurry, Scurry, Scurry. I'm sitting say about 3-4 seats away from Pat, who is next to Mullin, then Walter Berry, then Otis Thorpe, then Johnny Newman, then me. I am a New Yorker so they anticipated a package deal with Ewing and me.

The sweepstakes dwindled to the second round. The 37th pick rolled around and the Utah Jazz had the selection. That pick was Carey Scurry out of L.I.U. The crowd went silent with looks of shock on their faces. A hometown favorite not picked meant sending the Knicks fans home disappointed. The Knicks were beloved by New Yorkers and a most reputable franchise with two NBA Championships under its belt from '70 and '73. They'd lost some shine after that and Patrick Ewing was the franchise player who could restore its glory days. I have to admit I wanted to be one of the glory makers. I however was picked by the Utah Jazz and when my stats came out in the paper I felt legit.

- Name: Carey Scurry
- Position: Power Forward
- Height: 6-9 (2.05m)
- Weight: 205 (93kg)
- College Team: Long Island Blackbirds

- Nationality: American
- Birthplace: Brooklyn, New York
- Birthdate: 12/4/1962
- Drafted: Selected by the Utah Jazz in the second round (37th pick overall) of the 1985 NBA Draft.

Though disappointed I was not a home pick, I was elated to have been picked for the NBA. I sat a moment to take it in. Had my dream just come true? I, who couldn't even keep a passing academic grade was an NBA pick. I was sure all Mama's love and prayers, my brothers and sister, Doris's encouragement, and Grandma Ruth's belief that I was special were the driving forces against my fears that had allowed me to dream this dream. In the big scheme of things, this was a big deal. Of the 210 players who would be drafted in '85, I was one of them!

Once I was drafted, an escort appeared to take me to the back of the arena where a phone call from the Jazz coach Frank Layden was waiting for me to pick up. Frank broke the ice by telling me he too was from Brooklyn. He enthusiastically congratulated me on a job well done. Even though I didn't get drafted by the hometown team, I was drafted and I was potentially going to the NBA. After my initial disappointment, I was beyond excited. A draft does not mean certainty. It was time to earn my stripes.

The Utah Jazz, based in Salt Lake City, though not a top franchise like the Chicago Bulls or the Warriors, had qualified for their first playoff appearance in 1984, so in '85 I was walking into something good. My high school sweetheart and I were indeed about to live our dream come true. The nights we would sit up talking about this day had become a reality. One of my great joys was that I could help Mama now. My Mama whose love and protection would continue to save me from myself. But for her and my family, there would be no more hand-me-downs. All my hard work had paid off; the setbacks, the tears, the twisted ankles and injuries, and the night in and night out of practices were now reasons to celebrate. Even with failing academic grades, I had never given up on myself and I had to trust my God-given talent to see me through. My unshakable belief in myself had allowed me to face down all the challenges that came my way.

I exited the arena and stepped into my agent's limo waiting outside the arena. On my way home to share the good news with my family Rob gave me my congratulatory gifts; nips of Courvoisier and a pound of the best weed. Ron chauffeured me through the city as I pulled the sunroof back, got the bag, rolled up one, and exhaled smoke from the top-grade exotic weed. Pulling in front of the house, there was no red carpet treatment, only red eyes from the weed I was smoking but a crowd was gathered. I couldn't fit everybody in the limo, so I chose my brother Paul, whom I'd played college ball with and to whom I gave much of the credit for keeping me on the path of basketball, even after finding out he had a different agenda. Paul always knew he was never going pro. He would bring girls by to party and drink all night knowing I had to buckle down. I was on a different path. I did not want to jeopardize my basketball career so I'd slow my roll down a lot. We were not as close as we had been and he didn't seem to understand the pressure I was under. Paul, after playing for L.I.U. grew a life outside of basketball but he still found peace of mind in the evolving landscape of the game.

It's funny how life can change so fast. Before I left for Utah I spent a little time with my son. As usual, Doris my champion, was in my corner and knowing she'd bear the brunt of parenting, sent me off with a smile. I was offered a seventy thousand dollar non-guaranteed contract. It was more money than I had ever dreamed about! I had been signed with an option clause for $70,000 which meant if I made the team after tryouts, it would all be good. It would be the first money of this kind I had ever seen but the big word here was option. If I didn't make the team's final pick, my pleas for further consideration would fall on deaf ears and I'd be back on the auction block or back in the 'hood! I had to earn that promise.

I felt it would have been a distraction to take my young family with me to Utah, so I left them behind. I bid Doris a sad goodbye as I stepped into that limo for the third time, this time Utah-bound. Though sad to leave, I was on top of the world. People gathered in front of the tenement cheering and saying goodbye. Earl the Pearl fronted me a hundred bucks to tide me over until I got to Salt Lake City. I had only flown to Oklahoma and St Louis. The only times I had been out of the city previously were for the East vs. West Father's Day game in Washington, D.C., Oklahoma, Missouri, and Philly and I was ready to prove that I belonged. I was scared to death. Leaving home and everything familiar to me was challenging but this was a crucial moment in my life and I was about to step on the chariot that would take me to fame and fortune. Everything was new, an adventure, and I prayed I wouldn't mess up this time. Now, I just needed to do my part.

At J.F.K., I boarded a plane bound for Salt Lake City with a stopover in Chicago. I could hardly fit in the seat. People on the plane were checking me out, sure I was "somebody." By the time we arrived in Salt Lake, they probably had all figured out I must be one of the new players for The Jazz. After working all my life for this moment, I was off to the proving grounds. Time and effort would tell if I'd truly become a Jazz.

Utah is Mormon country and is mostly known for skiing. Well, I didn't do that. The place could not be more different than New York. Ultra-conservative, drugs and alcohol usage was frowned upon. Upon my arrival, Terry "T.C." Clark, the team trainer, met me and drove me to the Hilton Hotel on Main Street. There was no fanfare, no tour, it was all business. Terry was a tough, scared-straight kind of guy. I felt I was going to juvie instead of embarking on my professional career. I was reminded of what Mama used to say; I almost thought I could hear her voice in the back of my head saying, "They don't expect much, that's why so many young and eager ballers fail and go on to become criminals and addicts after not making it in the league." T.C. had seen a lot of guys come and go.

I was trying to strike up a conversation with him to feel things out. All he'd say was, "Just do your job." I began to wish I had listened to Mama. Her mantra was all work and no play. Education was first, and basketball was to be last. Here, basketball was my first and only choice and I was not feeling a warm and fuzzy welcome. But T.C. did his job…straight, no chaser!

Before the big money, we got a weekly stipend. I kept thinking about Doris. She was still living at home with her mother yet was down for mothering my son and was my biggest supporter. Through Mama, I sent Doris's support money regularly for her and Kaleef. I called her once a week, long distance. However, slowly we began to drift apart. Given the lifestyle of players, it'd be a miracle for relationships to survive. Although the calls were long distance, I called Mama sometimes three times a day. Mama would give me the usual pep talk; letting me know how proud she was and how I could do anything I put my mind to. All I had to hold onto were my Mama's belief in me and my outsized dream.

Camp was where all the players, free agents, recruits, and others came to get a chance at the ring. I had never been in such a stringent, professional sports environment. We were training in a small, hot gym that reminded me of our cramped Apt. 19 back home. Training was hard, demanding, and relentless. They counted every drop of sweat. Twice a day practices had players dropping like flies left and right. Some recruits would be called to the back of the gym by coaches never to be seen again. In 1985 there were fourteen NBA teams with fifteen players on each team. Thousands were waiting in the wings for a chance. If one failed here it opened up a spot for another hopeful.

Not knowing any of the other players on a first-name basis didn't help to loosen up the atmosphere. The first day of practice didn't help the situation either when so many people were dismissed. Tensions were high and I was determined. Each of us at camp was fighting for a spot on the team's lineup. Things got serious when it got down to the last twelve players. Players who were first picks and those from the previous season were already shoe-ins. These guys plus the successful camp tryouts would be the team roster to represent the Jazz Summer League. If I made the cut, I would be closer to becoming a Utah Jazz NBA player.

As a player with the Utah Jazz, I would make way more money than I ever could have back home, even if I could have gotten ten summer jobs. If chosen, from here on out there, I would have no worries in the world and a chance to have my name registered in the annals of basketball history. The reality of the basketball world is that every year new hot players are vying for a place on a team. On any given day, even if chosen, my position could be snatched right from under me. Guys were waiting in the wings for an opening to take my spot if I was injured and some guys were ready to just fucking beat you for your spot straight up. I gave them no reason to step to me.

The NBA deadline for the permanent roster was November 29th. I needed no distractions. It was close but not yet delivered. Jerry Sloan, the lead coach for the summer, was a rookie debuting himself as the team's head coach. He was coming off a successful basketball career as a hard-nosed player himself. An easygoing guy, he would end up being the third coach overall in the Jazz organization's history after my rookie year.

The only game face for the final twelve team members on the day of our first game was a look of worry. Everyone was wondering whose head was next on the chopping block. Players were sending their $400 per diem pocket money back home to show people they were chosen as if it was part of a contract. The contract was not real until we were really chosen. This left many of them fatigued from not eating properly. I wasn't going to let that happen to me. I needed all my strength from a full-course meal to make this dream happen. Being ready for the moment was what I knew as the Bed-Stuy "Do or Die" motto, and that meant I needed to be healthy.

The first game was exciting. We played the Sacramento Kings. We were equally matched. I was a small forward. The crowd knew me from the Summer League, so I'd already begun to build a fan base. They cheered as I did spectacular alley-oop dunks and held the best defense. I felt fierce. The Jazz wiped out the Kings and I'd made a good impression on the coaches, the team, and the fans. The Salt Lake fans would chant,"Scurry, Scurry, Scurry." I felt I had made it! I wish those chants had been enough.

The road to success is never smooth or easy and I soon found out that no news is good news. I'd been hearing through the grapevine that I was favored but I was still anxious when I heard no news. How would I make it to the veteran's camp if I didn't know what the coach was looking for in the team? I began a project homework. I learned everything I could about the team's needs. I tried to find out what they were looking for in a player. What they needed was a player who could get to the rim in the small forward position. I was the perfect fit. This intel allowed me to focus on my primary goal of being around the basket so I could do what I did best, rebound. I also found out that I was drafted based on the recommendation of Scott Layden, who happened to be an assistant coach for two years at Fairleigh Dickerson University. He'd told his dad, Frank Layden, who was the coach of the Jazz, that I was what they were looking for. A style of play that would fit the new blood coming into the season with their 1st round pick Karl "the Mailman" Malone. A legit 6'9' power forward who could deliver, Karl and teammate John Stockton would later rise as the team's franchise players and together formed one of the most famed offensive pick-and-roll teams in the history of the NBA.

Veterans camp was weeks away and things got down to the wire. Who would be next to go home? I was used to running the clock so I felt secure. Sloan was spending more time with me pushing me a little harder and using me as the poster child for demonstrating plays to my fellow teammates which was a good sign. I was advanced defense-wise, it was my specialty. My teammates looked up to me. The same attention I got at L.I.U. transferred to the summer league. My credentials turned heads and I was catching jaw-dropping alley-oops from Alfredrick Hughes, Delany Rudd, and Gonzaga, who was an already settled player from the previous year. I had led the Blackbird in every category, and I was ready to use what was in my toolbox to the fullest extent for the Jazz.

In the final summer league against Tom Chambers, Pace Mannion, Fred Roberts, Danny Shayes, and Fred Hayes I was amazed that indeed The Jazz would draft me. Finally, chosen, I was offered a one-year contract for seventy thousand. My number was 22. Funny how when my pick was confirmed, people who passed me on the street claimed to be friends. Everyone wanted to be remembered.

I donned my Jersey ready to battle it out against some of the best players in the country and it was showtime. My first home game as a Utah Jazz was exciting. For real the stadium was electric. Pom-Pom shaking Cheerleaders and Jazz Bear, the Jazz mascot would whip the crowd into a frenzy before we trotted out onto the court. In attendance, right in the front row, were Pistol Pete, one of ball's great ball handlers, who would die three years later of heart failure, John Denver the country singer, and the Osmond Brothers. It was heady! The whole of Utah State had no choice but to come out to see for themselves if what they'd heard about these new Jazzmen coming to their town was real.

There was a lot of money riding on us but at the moment it had no value in comparison to the game we needed to play. I for one, wanted more. I wanted my game to be rock solid and though it would have been a dream come true to have played for my home team Knicks, I'd made the cut at Veterans Camp and fulfilled my dream of playing in the NBA.

I doubled down on my game and I gave it everything I had to give. I left veterans camp a legitimate Utah Jazz team member though the permanent roster would not be announced until November 29. Karl Malone, and power forward John Stockton, a first round pick by the Jazz from the Gongaza Bulldogs were a surety. That left thirteen spots to fill. The day for permanent draft picks rolled around and as expected I made it! I didn't have to worry about anything else at this point, I was signed. Rickey Green took me under his wing. He was a 6-year NBA veteran from Chicago and he taught me how the organization was run off the court. Their image had no tolerance for bad publicity and I followed his instructions.

Larry H. Miller owned the Jazz and half of Salt Lake City. He wielded power much like Mr. Bill did when I was at Oklahoma Junior College. With a few car dealerships in his portfolio, he furnished us with demo cars that would be at our disposal when needed. I had no driver's license and was tooling around without one. With my profile so high and Rickey Green's image lesson in my head, I couldn't take the risk, so as a savvy streetwise person, I paid $100 under the table to get one. Within an hour, I had every document, including a driver's license, available to become a fully legitimate citizen.

The NBA season was finally underway. I was going to have to share time with Darrell Griffith, 2 Guard, and Bobby Hanson, also a 2 Guard. They shifted my time on the court, as they were more experienced. Although I shone during practice, they had seniority during the game. They look the lead. The first few games were a learning experience for all the rookies, just waiting for their turn to debut. In my rookie year, I averaged 4.7 points, 3.1 rebounds, 1.1 assists, 1 steal, and 0.8 blocks per game.

A moment I remember clearly was from my rookie season. We were going to play an away game against the Knicks. I was going home and family and friends came out in droves and took up half the stadium to see me play. That day was the test of all tests. I was excited to be home and I wanted to shine. Before the game though, I was told that I probably would not be playing since the coach didn't want me to get too excited and make mistakes. I was crushed. As coach was explaining his rationale to me I felt the wind seeping out of my sails. To this day I still don't buy that shit the coach told me. Had he been so concerned about my making a mistake, if I were prone to getting excited, a good coach would have given me a heads up to let me know he'd be watching out for signs of that kind of behavior if he put me on the court. This was my hometown! To this day, I believe that one moment brought my stock and my enthusiasm for the Jazz down. The Jazz would disappoint me in my rookie year.

During the game, the crowd of my peers grew angry and Coach Layden was signaling my people to calm down. The team members, who might have softened my blow did not rally around me. It was a dog-eat-dog world. Everyman for himself. We were a mixed team of six Black players and six White players. Where we came together seamlessly was on the court. We were one team but we all gravitated to similar people. I hung out with the Black players, Karl Malone, Thurl Bailey, Rickey Greene, Darrell Griffith, and Dell Curry.

From that day on, I lost respect for the Jazz organization and knew I wanted out. After having a successful rookie year, however, I signed a new multi-million-dollar contract for three more years. I was mad as hell but I was not about to bite the hand that fed me and my family. Not yet. No matter how unhappy I was, given where

I came from, I would be a fool to turn down a multi-million dollar contract, but with stipulations over my head, it would determine my fate as a Jazzman.

And if I looked back, it was a day that subliminally permitted me to slip into darkness. It was a day that reminded me that no matter how hard I tried, a White man held my destiny. No one knew what I could have done had the N.Y. Knicks drafted me, but I truly believe the Knicks would have taken my career to the next level. This lack of confidence and belief in a player can make morale nonexistent. I should have gauged the team's attitude from my lackluster welcome. Naturally, it was erroneous thinking, but when you've been derailed so many times by race in America it's hard to understand that no one held my destiny but me. To deal with the disappointment I used drugs to mellow out.

— EIGHT —

MONEY COMES AND MONEY GOES

That $70,000 came and went overnight. With money flowing, suddenly you become the banker for a lot of folks. I had to pay dues to the organization and my agent, Joe Glass. My responsibility to my family was tearing me apart as well. I was Santa Claus all year round. Strapped for cash, I probably had $35,000 left from my contract. I purchased a legal firearm in Utah after hearing the word out on the mean streets of Brooklyn, was that I was making millions. I knew my neighborhood and if I was going to be there I needed to protect myself.

Getting off the plane at JFK, I would take a shuttle to Avis's car rental, get my favorite Lincoln Town Car then return to get my luggage. Airport authorities approached me when I returned because they saw the gun in my luggage through the security X-ray detector. I had a Utah permit but New York had restrictions on assault weapons required additional permits to cross state lines with them.

I was scared at the moment, but I was never charged because of my status as a player, and the fact that I had a Utah gun permit in the box with the gun. It so happened that Marc Lavaroni, my teammate at the Jazz's father was working that shift at JFK. Still, this was strike negative one when the organization got wind of it.

It was the mid-to-late eighties. Drugs were in vogue from Wall Street to main streets and you could find it anywhere in the hoods. No one knew the addictive powers of these drugs at the time, it was the in thing to do. A little rattled and needing to check out for a bit, I took the Major Deegan Expressway over at the Grand Concourse until I reached the Bronx Expressway then crossed over the GW Bridge to 181st and Amsterdam Avenue. I was now in Washington Heights, known as the drug capital of N.Y. The dealers I knew operated out of a tenement building, apartment 5F. After being held for hours at the airport 'holding pen,' I couldn't wait to unwind. My way of unwinding was snorting coke, my drug of choice since I'd graduated from weed as my relaxation choice. I wanted to score a dime of coke. I knew I was already bringing old behaviors into my new life which didn't mix but I thought I was in control.

Three Dominicans were conducting business. The one who called me over was a steerer (the steerer tells the buyer where to go to buy drugs), the second was the server (the person doing the drug transaction) and the third was carrying large automatic weapons (the shooter and the bodyguard). There were clear differentiations of the roles in the drug trade. At that time, Harlem was the most dangerous, crime-ridden place in the city, but Washington Heights was the daddy of drug dealing. It was around the time when crack hit the streets. Crack got its name from the crackling sound made when cocaine mixed with baking soda was being cooked, turning the mixture into a harder compound. Crack cocaine would go on to decimate Black neighborhoods in ways no one ever imagined. Highly addictive, it turned people into zombies and it was making street millionaires by the boatload. Crack would go on to sweep through the Black neighborhoods like a tornado and in its wake it would leave destruction never before seen or imagined. The magic drug that could ease the pain of debilitating pasts was in itself the most incapacitating of them all. I wanted no part of that.

The dealers were waiting for the exchange. Dealing with that much money, any wrong move and things could go downhill. I knew a little Spanish from my days in the southside of Williamsburg so I asked for a sample of coke in Spanglish to calm the vibe of the room—of any suspicion that I might be an undercover cop. The first dealer said, *"Primo, a mi Nomi importa el dinero pito, este tipo esto diciendo. Que Juega Baloncesto professional en TV conocess?* ("Cousin, I don't care about the money," this guy was saying. "What do you know about professional basketball on TV?") The 2nd dealer said, *"No lo conosco, ni mi importa conocerlo."* Then he screamed out loud, *"Avansa!, "Que hace este tipo aqui. Vamos a ver si es verdad que est a limpio dejalo que fumo que coja un fuergo."* ("I don't know him, nor do I care to know him." "Avansa, what's this guy doing here? Let's see if it's true that he's clean, let him smoke, let him take a cigar.) I sampled the goods and stashed my score before leaving that spot.

I'd heard about fake cops robbing customers of their merchandise, even stripping them of their clothes. The dealers themselves were warning me to be mindful. I wondered how fake those cops really were. Real cops, many recruited from distressed neighborhoods for their last chance of success, knew the game only too well. It wasn't hard to create a crooked cop in the neighborhood they were supposed to protect. As the saying goes, you can't make a silk purse out of a sow's ear. As for me, the amount of coke I brought afforded me a safe trip out of the 'hood from the lookouts and I made it to 125th Street. A block from the F.D.R., I pulled over for another hit. The first one I took at the dealer's apartment had opened the floodgates back up. The thing about cocaine is the high only lasts for twenty minutes or so, so to keep feeling invincible it requires more and more to flood the brain with dopamine—the carefree, happy hormone.

The area of Harlem I was driving through was populated with street walkers looking for company but even the squalid neighborhood was serene. Of all the boroughs of blight, Harlem was legendary. Harlem was considered part of Manhattan until the renaissance of the Black influx in the 30s. It became a literary Mecca for Black artists such as Langston Huges, Zora Neale Hurston, and James Van Der Zee and spawned what became known as the Harlem Renaissance—a revival of the intellectual and cultural hub where African American literature, music, dance, theater, art, and fashion flourished. The once majestic blocks lined with old brownstones and nineteenth-century buildings were now in disrepair and looked impassable.

It was 5:00 p.m. and I had not yet seen my family. Was I in a rush? Not with twenty-five grams of cocaine in my pocket. Hitting the F.D.R., listening to Heavy D., and looking for a shortcut, passing Fort Green projects on the Brooklyn Queens Expressway (B.Q.E.), I quickly pulled onto Nostrand Avenue. I was at arm's length from Clifton Place. The usuals were on the corner just like I'd left them, hanging around Frank's Barber Shop. Nothing had changed.

Staying in the far-right lane, so as not to be noticed, I blinked my signal to make the quick left on Greene Avenue. I knew if they had seen me, I wouldn't have made it home. I parked on Greene Avenue in front of Casino Mike's home. Casino Mike was a "made" man from the 'hood. Everybody respected him. He had my back even when I was at L.I.U. and was someone I could count on. By this time, I had copped another gun in the 'hood, a 22-caliber pistol from the bodega on the corner. Casino Mike took it from me saying I didn't need it cause as usual he had my back. At that moment, I had a pass to go anywhere in the five boroughs.

I adhered to the street creed "If you have it, flaunt it." I was wearing a large nugget ring and a 30-inch, 24-karat gold chain flanked with diamonds around a pyramid with Scurry embedded in the middle. I was flashy enough to draw the wolves out. Walking back to the block, I noticed detectives asking questions about an unsolved murder of a transgender named Robert who owned a beauty salon on Nostrand Avenue. I kept going. Finally, I reached the steps of our apartment, stopping off on the 3rd floor where my sister Linda had her apartment, just downstairs from Mama. I gave her and my nieces a few bucks. I dropped off the coke and a few hundred dollars at my apartment in the same building in preparation to visit Mama on the 4th floor. I was doing all I could to be perceived as the good son. There was no way I could let Mama know I was caught up in drugs. I had been using drugs for a while but I didn't realize I was now becoming dependent on it to function. As the pressure to deliver for the Jazz and my family increased, I was using more and more to escape.

The coke started taking its toll on me and paranoia set in. I had used so much I couldn't sit long enough to hold a decent conversation with Mama. I had to come up with an excuse about meeting my agent so I could leave Mama's place in a hurry. I promised her I would be back and I hightailed it out of there knowing I would be downstairs for three days feeling guilty and getting high. I had to return to Mama with composure.

About now I should have known I was spiraling but instead of sitting out the high, I went to Rand's Liquor Store right up the block on Bedford Avenue to get a bottle to calm down from the coke high. The coke made me feel grand, like the king I was supposed to be. I made sure the money I had was super obvious. No way anyone who saw me could doubt I was rolling in dough. I had only been gone a year, and everybody I'd left behind looked like new money too. It was the crack era and people were printing money. My consolation, my money was legit. Hip-hop was changing too and would in the late 80s and early 90s soon give rise to more hardcore protest music, Gangsta rap. Thugs roamed the streets in B.V.D.'s otherwise known as men's long underwear of all colors which was the rage. Lee jeans, Pumas, and 69ers were signature for these playboys and they had them all. 'Hood fabulous was what I admired about these dudes on the block. 'Hood trends would later become a culture unto itself and when hip-hoppers adopted Chukkas as a status symbol, brands like Timberland boots, exploded and became a household name.

No way would I have considered myself an addict. I was just a product of my time and everybody who was somebody was doing coke from Wall Street to the mean streets. But soon my new behavior became embedded within me and the complicated dance with addiction began. In the late '80s, ball players wanted to be hustlers and the hustlers wanted to be ball players. There was money in both games but those lives weren't meant to be synonymous. The drug game was booming and it was all about the Benjamins. Damn near everything was free enterprise. The game was to be sold, not told, by the truckload. Rolling in vintage Caddies, old series BMWs, and 5.0 Benzes, music pumping from speakers several decibels too loud, street hustlers were everywhere. Boys with boom boxes on sidewalks played Doug E. Fresh, Grand Master Flash, and other popular songs for the B-boys hustling their breakdancing. Others simply just roamed the street with their boom boxes on their shoulders like Radio Raheem did in Spike Lee's, *Do The Right Thing*.

It became clear that the reason coke was getting cheaper was because there was plenty of it. Crack was becoming the new ghetto drug. In my mind, I was dabbling with drugs to chill and release pressure, totally unaware that this intentional sabotage was by design to turn the Black community on its head. My fortune was to be made with the NBA, but I was spending it in the streets.

There were still two months before I had to head back to Utah. I went looking for old friends. I was observing what crack was doing to people I knew and I stayed clear of it. My seeking out my friends caught the attention and raised the eyebrows of well-known gangsters like I-God, Homicide, T-Rock, and Puerto Rican Supreme. These guys were hardcore "gangstas" with little to no regard for anything or anybody, other than the Benjamins that rolled in like a river. Money was good in the 'hood. The newly minted street millionaires needed a place to spend their money so gambling became a big deal. Holding dice games, attracting high rollers, and placing big bets with stakes in the thousands was their game. I of course wanted in.

I went in a little over my head, and that put me in a bind with a known killer named Redbug. I was also running up a drug tab around a rack of one thousand dollars a day or more and because of this and gambling, had an IOU out to Redbug. Redbug was no joke. He was known for brandishing guns: hammers, burners, biscuits, toolies, and the grip…all names for different types of guns in the 'hood. When I was late with my I.O.U. dough, Redbug, not one to play, arrived at Mama's doorstep looking for his money. He and his thugs had come to collect. They knocked on the front door and explained to Mama that she needed to pay up for my debt. Mama gave them enough money so they wouldn't harm my brothers and sisters…or even her. Thugs will stop at nothing and spare no one to collect monies owed at any time or any place and they will make their presence known. It wasn't all I owed but Mama's money had them satisfied enough to give me a chance to figure out the rest. My gambling had almost cost our family another tragedy. I urgently needed help in more ways than I was thinking. I turned to Casino Mike, who fronted me the money with interest, and the day was saved. My brother Dale was furious. He hated that I was mingling with drug dealers and killers. Dale was so very upset with me, that he hardly spoke to me. But I was not in the drug trade. I was the only one not in the drug trade with real paper, and I believed the 'hood motto, "If you got it, flaunt it."

I should have realized then that my life was headed to the abyss but this was my 'hood. As the vulgar saying goes, "You can take the nigga out of the 'hood, but you can't take the 'hood out of the nigga." I ignored all the signs of trouble. I felt terrible most of the time about my behavior, but I was out of control. While I was becoming a 'hood phenom there was also controversy swirling about me not only at home but in the locker rooms and halls of the NBA. I was nothing but a drughead.

Because of my drug use, I infrequently saw Doris and Kaleef. Doris abhorred my use of drugs and the people I hung out with. I ignored her and my son as much as I ignored my family's warnings. I didn't care. Drugs thought for me and were beginning to rule my life. Somewhere deep inside though I felt the warning even if I didn't give it the time of day.

But it was time to get my act together. I had to get a grip before returning to Utah, which was now only a month away. I called my JAZZ teammates Karl, Thurl, and Rickey for us to come up with a plan to get back in shape so we could be at our best and in peak shape when we returned. Sensing the danger even if not fully understood, I would therefore go back to Utah early, a little rawer than when I had left. I didn't just need to get in shape, I needed rehabilitation. After passing the drug test with flying colors, I was ready for the team's physical. I again passed with flying colors. I kept fooling myself I could handle both—the game and the drugs.

The next year was magical for me. John Stockton joined the team as a first-draft pick point guard. John and I had synergy. The team executed fast breaks, alley-opps, pick and roll strategies with deftness. So here we were, a homeboy from Brooklyn, a country kid from Summerfield, Louisiana, and a fighting Irish (Me, Karl, John) dominating the court. That year we were welcomed as prodigal sons to the Mormon state. Utah had gotten its confirmation.

After signing my contract, I moved out of the hotel and into the Trolley Square Apartments. It was a downtown complex similar to the Louis Armstrong Projects. At this time, I was comfortable enough and decided to send for my young family, Doris, and Khaleef. Everything was brand new. Doris had always been a stabilizing force for me and maybe with my son there I would feel more inclined to get my act together. But temptation that promises so many feel-good times was hard to turn down.

If I was a catch for women back home as a college player, I was gold for women who are determined to date a drafted ball player and diamond for those determined to marry one. It was insane. Groupies to a player came a dime a dozen and too often I was thinking with the wrong head. I foolishly had a one-night stand right under Doris's nose with a girl from whom I got a tingling and burning sensation from unprotected sex. This time I got into big trouble health-wise and Doriswise. That woman gave me an STD. Doris was livid. The team doctor gave me a shot that stung throughout my body. Never again was I ever going down that road! After having our first argument, I decided to send Doris and Khaleef back home. In reality, I was not prepared to be a partner or a parent. Fame and money in my pocket were getting to my head and the lurking demons were only too happy to join the dance.

One morning in July 1987, my third season with the Jazz, Coach Layden advised me to stay in Utah for the summer league so I could work on my game. This came from the top dogs who were afraid of a repeat of the mistake the coach had pulled in N.Y. I was again wondering if I wanted to be traded, and I did. I decided to head to Brooklyn before the summer league started and super early before veteran's camp, three months away. At that time, I stopped hanging out with Karl Malone and all the positive influences around me. I was jealous of their contracts being renewed with many more benefits while mine always seemed to hang in uncertain status. Their life was set, but for me, I had to prove myself once again. I was facing down fear once again and I was beginning to feel like a failure.

Unfortunately, this behavior became a pattern of drugging and figuring out how to pass the tests for the next two seasons. The court became my jester's stage. My drug use began to take a serious toll and I was in the throes of addiction. I was hoping and hoping against hope that no one had noticed a difference in my behavior, but I was only fooling myself. I thought I was so slick because I could get past Utah's detectors.

We were opening our first home game after returning from a long road trip West against Reggie Theus and the Sacramento Kings. The Kings were the oldest team in the NBA, and the first team in the major professional North American sports leagues. Their standing, however, was always a challenge. We solidly beat them and that same night, I started to celebrate too early. Bombarded by women and free drinks it was a night to remember.

Excited about our future, Karl and I would spend the entire night discussing what we would do in the future. I really liked Karl though I'd distanced myself. Having faced down his own issues, not drug-related, he was compassionate to my plight. Karl was a company man and serious about his career. I figured if I stayed around him I would pull myself up. He for sure had a future and I wanted to make sure I did too.

One night at a Houston Rockets game, the drama of my drug use played out on the court and the inevitable happened. An in-game incident woke up the whole state. Carey Scurry missed an alley-oop. "It was like a classical, tragic Greek play," the way Stockton would write it. Stockton and I were a dream team. Stockton and I had this one play that would electrify the crowd. Stockton would give me the look and tap his leg. I would signal my readiness to go to the hoop with a return tap. This is how he became the assist king and us an indomitable ally-oop team. That night, Stockton executed his customary signal of tapping his leg, my cue to be ready. I got the cue and tapped back. It was a perfect pass but I fumbled the ball, couldn't hold on to it, and lost it to the Houston Rockets. My coordination and timing were so off because of my indulgence in drugs for several nights before that game. Unfortunately, drugs can take days to get out of your system. I thought I had a way of camouflaging my drug use but it got the better of me that night. As a result, Stockton never looked my way again. The magic was gone. I had broken his trust and that of the team. I had failed to be a team player because of my drug use.

I wasn't the only drug abuser. The NBA had a drug problem. Do you have any idea of how many pro athletes got high? I'm not just talking about weed or booze either. Still, the fact that I was not willing to admit that my life was unmanageable doesn't mean that it wasn't.

The coke use in the league had gotten real bad, so they stepped up their drug testing. We'd usually be tested only during the off-season. Now they were picking random days during the season to test us. The Len Bias tragedy was the last straw for the league. Two days after being selected by the Boston Celtics, Bias died from cardiac arrhythmia induced by a cocaine overdose. They were trying to pinpoint the coke users in the league to protect their image and they felt it was mostly the Black players who were the offenders. Black players were expendable; the inner city produced them by the hundreds! These random tests proved that White players were drugging as much as anyone else. They stopped doing as much drug testing soon after because it started affecting the White players.

A few stories were swept under the rug, such as Tom Chambers's excessive drinking. For Chris Mullins and Bobby Hansen's drug use, they used alcohol as a front for a 30-day rehab. No surprise that in America it's impossible to get away from race. Meanwhile, for the same offense Blacks were blackballed. David Thompson, Ray Richardson, Roy Tarpley, John Drew, John Lucas, George Gervin, Bernard King, and others I knew from police reports were all involved.

Some players were using high-quality drugs and were not worried about the consequences. It was a sign of the times.

John Lucas would later be an ace for me. There was no real intervention program for athletes. I think mostly because no one knew the full extent of this kind of addiction. This acceptable widespread social drug usage was something new.

The problem was that Black players too ignored the growing trend of Len Bias like deaths as being a red flag. I certainly didn't take a cue from "there but for the grace of God go I," Len Bias's story could have been mine. I needed to get myself some help. Not even my fumbling of the ball and the direct indication that could end my career stopped me in my tracks though. Instead, I began camouflaging my usage with an up-tempo attitude. I was spending a little over $2,000 on coke during the "87-'88 season, using fancy coke bottles with a spoon attached to them. Nobody wanted to address the growing issue of drugs. While cocaine might have been more prevalent among Black players, alcohol, and lots of it, was the little white lie for White players. It was okay to have alcohol in the locker room, but teams were not accepting of the Black drug of choice, coke.

My playing time started to fluctuate and my game faltered. I was missing defensive calls and I lacked concentration. I wasn't the old fierce defensive player…I wasn't Scurry. Drugs were controlling me. I was spending more time on the bench. Delusional, I questioned the coach's decision, which drew more attention to my deteriorating state. I was trying to defend myself…everybody could see it but me, that I was no longer in control. Rickey Green, a first-draft pick from the University of Michigan and my old buddy had been the first one to pull me aside to tell me about image. Now my image was suffering beyond repair. This time when he again pulled my coattail it was to tell me that when stuff like this happens and the coach pulls back on a player, a trade is usually in the air. Players are traded all the time and for a variety of reasons, one being to improve the team and get rid of its weakest link. A trade was in the air but it turned out Adrian Dantley was being traded to Detroit Pistons for Kelly Tripuka. Other trades were coming left and right. Larry H. Miller, the owner of the team at the time, wanted a whole new look for Jazz. New uniforms and a new future. This was business as usual, a part I had to get used to. The shooting guard position, also known as the "2", was loaded and I felt like cattle as opposed to being a member of a franchise. I could be replaced at any minute and it was clear I was expendable.

We were going into the season with new faces and our veteran, Mark Eaton, was at the end of his career with two bad knees. Our season record was unexplainable at barely above the .500 mark. Going into the '86-'87 playoffs, we were slotted to play against Golden State Warriors. We lost the best of 5 series 3-2 in the Salt Palace and I felt the tension in the air of the city after the playoffs. This was a city that would embrace us as Gods when we were winning but now turned on us. When Karl and I would go to our favorite restaurant that summer, it seemed like they wanted to destroy the very silverware we used. Their horses were lame and were ready to be put out to pasture.

Utah was no less racist than Oklahoma and even the team had its share of segregation between the six White players and the six Black players. It was all about money, power, and no respect for players. We were simply chattel, the White players less so than the Black players. Rick would leave the Jazz the following year in 1992. Both John and Malone would leave Jazz but not until 2004.

— NINE —

DITCH EFFORT

I needed to redeem myself. Playing the Knicks for the last time on our West Coast road trip, I wanted and needed the chance to show my assets in front of the team that wanted me from the beginning. My ego and morale needed it. I'd also found out that Rick Pitino had wanted me in N.Y. to begin with because he knew right away the Utah Jazz weren't going to pay me my worth. This was my chance if I wanted to be traded to the Knicks. I didn't mind Utah at first since Karl 'The Mailman' Malone and I were starting together and having John in it the second year was rewarding.

That game again, Coach Frank thought it would be in my best interest not to play me. Surely he'd put me in even for a few minutes. He had to. I sat patiently waiting. Rickey, Thurl, and Karl all felt for me. The fans too anticipated that at some point in time, he would put me in. Maybe halftime…nope.

Fourth quarter, nope.

One minute left, nope.

I had to develop a thick skin to be in the basketball business. As much as Coach Frank wasn't playing me, he still wouldn't let me go when the Knicks inquired about a deal with me that was supposed to go down in exchange for a few players. If not me as the one, who would be traded? Louis Orr, Trent Tucker, Kenny Walker, Johnny Newman? I was the deal trade Pitino had requested at the beginning of the season, but Jazz had no intention of letting me go. Behind the whole ordeal, I can still recall a ref's racist comment about "how lucky I was to be employed there." Mark Eaton was a Californian who like me had attended Automotive School. He was a towering 7'4" white guy who'd been a 4th pick for the Jazz where he played for his entire career. Mark had overheard the coach's racist remark and at halftime came over to explain that the ref had apologized for his words. Yeah, but he didn't apologize to me. What Mark was really doing was hoping I wouldn't report the referee to the league authorities for his racist remarks. But that shit made me realize, as Michael Jackson would sing a few years later, *They Don't Care About Us.* You can't be Black in America and not be subjected to racist remarks.

I was quiet in the locker room and distanced myself from the team. Once I reached home, I complained to my agent that I wanted to be traded. The Utah Jazz could very well be my kryptonite and I wanted out. They had no choice after my incident with Mel Turpin and the gun fiasco at the airport. I was being sidelined anyway. Turpin was a sixth overall pick in the 1984 draft who would later commit suicide. The 6' 7' center from Kentucky, with whom I had a physical altercation because he accused me of being disrespectful to his wife.

As a consolation, I moved to a new and upgraded bachelor pad, Woodbine Condo, where I felt like I had more peace. More peace meant less drug use and I wanted to reign that in. Woodbine was a sleepy residence further from the downtown area of Trolley Square where I used to be. The neighbors seem to have taken my move all in stride. I was an exception. A Utah Jazz. As I walked around the upper-class neighborhood, I was so out of my comfort zone. People around me moved in a slow deliberate fashion. They were accustomed to never being in a hurry as they never worried about dodging bullets or running for their lives. Life was just too sedate. It was hard enough to find a pusher man in Utah—a no-drug, no-alcohol state at least culturally—and here in the neighborhood it was impossible.

I decided to ask Helen, one of the two Blacks who lived in the area, some questions. Helen was a clerk at the First National Bank and Leon was the barber Karl and I frequented for our haircuts. Alienated and feeling the sting of racism I needed to be around my people. The summer before going into the '87-'88 season, I found out where the Blacks were isolated in Utah, thirty-five miles away. As Helen and I walked along the downtown streets, she gave me directions and a word of caution. I, not prone to listening to anyone, did not heed her words of caution.

The peeps in this 'hood may not have been in a hurry but I was. I withdrew $2,500 from the First National Bank and headed toward Ogden. Listening to Alexander O'Neal in my borrowed 4x4 Blazer Jeep, I was back in the 'hood. I immediately recognized the swagger. As I exited off a ramp right to the center of the hood, I noticed some people gathered around a chicken joint and some leaning against the wall. Mothers were towing their small children. Young girls and boys moving slowly but deliberately in their slinking way were all too familiar. There's something about Black communities everywhere. It hums with a vibe. As they would say water seeks its own level and I could feel the connection. Some things never change. Like attracts like and I was one of them. I was beginning to feel comfortable and a bit more confident that I could pull off what I came for. A little calming substance to deal with feeling alienated. I was not winning with the drugs.

I knew the streets. They were now checking me out as much as I was checking them out. Could I hear their minds or was it mine making all that noise? Once I got closer, what would I say?

"What's happening?" I said lazily to anybody interested.

"Hey, you, what's happening," said a short, stocky guy with a jerry curl. I thought of Rick James. His name was Charles. He was smiling and so were the others.

I broke the ice. "Where's the" white girl?" I asked using the slang for cocaine.

"Right here." Charles's girl was White. "You left yourself open for that," Charles said, grinning. He couldn't pass that one up. "Where are you from?" he asked.

"From New York," I said. But I couldn't reveal my true identity as a Jazz player and he didn't seem to know who I was. But, he knew why I was there. He told me I could ask anybody I saw on the street about him and his credibility. As the night fell upon us, an invitation to a club was offered. We pulled into a tight parking lot that had the capacity of 100 and that was pushing it. Charles was in an interracial relationship which only drew more attention to him. There was nothing wrong with these sisters, but hey, more Black sisters for me!

Utah's downtown nightlife, when we could get in on the weekends, required that I wear the suit of a Mr. Bojangles. In the affluent neighborhoods, I was used to answering a sidebar of trivia questions, and even having to sign autographs at lunch before I could swallow my food was the norm. Life in the 'hood was different. Taking my mask off at the end of the season wasn't without trial and error.

After my fumble, Stockton lost faith in me. Attendance to games dwindled because the fans didn't have enough of my high-flying alley-oops passed from the best guard in the N.B.A., John Stockton, to the Dog, a nickname given to me by Jeff Wilkens, a player from Chicago's West side. I was the one in the players' space like a pit bull on 'em, but I was no longer trusted. Worst, my contract was on the brink of renewal. Not knowing that in the coach's eyes, I had passed for the next season with flying colors. I was sweating it.

It was a short summer and we needed to get practice for the upcoming '87 season just around the corner. I decided to shoot home for a few weeks to see my family. We'd only come to the East division on a seven-game road trip so I didn't see them often. The war on poverty had certainly failed Bed-Stuy. The depravity and desperation of the hood remained the same, if not escalated but it was what I knew inside and out. Even after my cushy apartment in Utah, home was home. Even with all the chaos of drive-bys, robberies, murders, and assaults, I knew these streets. Having money put me in a different league anyway and afforded me a V.I.P. pass to Bed-Stuy's most shady if exclusive places. One such, Club 432, a place where shot callers dwelled would play heavily in my demise. They were the big boys who indeed called the shots—mob bosses, big heavy-weight dealers, pimps, serious hustlers. Only the cream of the very rotten crop could roll up to a place like Club 432. The code to get in was to ring the bell twice. The doormen, whom I later came to know as Zip and Corb, would open up the heavily bolted doors and they were armed. Stone-faced as hell, I knew I was in business—they were all young Black dudes and I was Carey Scurry. Looking back, I wish I had skipped that day at the club.

Watching the draft that night from Club 432 on Nostrand Avenue I heard the announcer, David Stern, calling my name. As I raised a spoon to my nose, I thought they'd finally decided to end my career. I knew I was on slippery slopes. Mistakenly, it wasn't Carey Scurry, but Dell Curry. I decided I had to talk to my agent, Joe Glass, about being signed or traded before I was next. I called Joe.

"I think you should come out to Woodmere, Long Island," Joe said. Wasted, it seemed like hours of driving to get there even though it was only about fifteen miles away. Woodmere might only have been fifteen minutes away but it could have been Mars, it was so different from Bed-Stuy. The predominantly Jewish neighborhood is known as one of the best places to live in New York and flush with money, money. Joe opened the door and invited me in. I go in and sit down. For a long time, I didn't respond to anything he said. As he spoke I wondered why I, the talent was in Bed-Stuy, and he, my agent was in Woodmere…it was all about options and opportunities—the quality of the straw you draw. He was now rehashing the what-ifs: The doors that had been left open; Washington Bullets, Detroit Pistons, L.A Lakers. Jerry West an NBA executive and former Lakers had all approached me in the recruiting era back then, but now all those doors were slamming shut. "They would not touch you, now," Joe proclaims. "You're too risky. It's the N.B.A.'s policy. For right now, I think you should hold on to what you got." That sounded very strange coming from him. Joe had always been there for me, but now he sounded unsure.

I'd said to him on several occasions that I thought I might be more effective somewhere else. Some place where my talent could grow and I would be appreciated. Not being signed yet made me even more paranoid than the drugs. I left feeling no better than when I came…maybe even a little worse.

After that, wallowing in self-pity and throwing my own pity party I started coming home in the wee hours of the morning, always dreading the approach of dawn. Mama was no fool and whether in the light of day or not, she could see right through my façade. Mama would have a disgusted look on her face. She saw something I didn't see back then, which was me sliding backward. She would talk until she was blue in the face and I couldn't hear it, always denying the obvious.

At this time of the crack era, which I hadn't experienced yet, my drug of choice was coke and lots of it, and though it was becoming an issue, I was safe from the zombie-like effects of crack that rendered some of the people I knew into derelicts beyond recognition. I would look at them and shake my head in disbelief that so and so… was now a crackhead.

At the club, Zip and Corb remained fierce. They'd let me into the club without even a smile. No matter how many times I saw them, I couldn't tell you a single thing about them. In a situation like that, you don't stare people down. I was there to make friends, not enemies. Over at the bar, I would order a drink to ease the tension of all eyes being on me. Looking over at a fine chick who it seemed nobody was paying attention to, I asked her name. Kathy was phat, I mean she was gorgeous. I couldn't believe a girl like her would be caught dead in a hell hole like this but looks are deceiving. She was looking hard at my diamond rings and asked me if they were real. Was I the catch of the day? I was down with that. Kathy pulled out some shit right in front of me and took a toot, one-one of coke. My type of girl. The night looked promising. "Let's get out of here," I said, but she just sat there. I started to have a bad feeling about this conversation. I soon found out why. Kathy was the boss's girl. She was with it until Mr. Carter, the Big Boss, walked in from the back room. I guess she was too scared to move. Carter was somebody I knew from the 'hood who had done some time. I backed way off. I wasn't looking for trouble.

Someone in the club was bragging to people about plotting to rob me, but that didn't happen because my new friends and lookouts were dealers, addicts, and chicken heads (hookers). These cats had my back and were looking out for me, especially since I could pay. Hanging at the club, my life was becoming unmanageable. I started chasing coke. How could this have happened to me? Now I was owing people or running coke tabs exceeding $1,000 a day.

Finally, and luckily the call I was waiting for came. I got news about my new contract worth multi-millions on a 3-year deal. I contacted Karl about our return to Utah to start our preparation for our physical. Well, at least for him it would be no big deal. Karl didn't mess around. He was all about the game. On the other hand, I had to get my system cleaned out! Jerry Sloan, a veteran who had played in the NBA for eleven seasons was the new coach for the Utah Jazz. He was no-nonsense and wanted to make sure we stayed focused on my game. His eye was on me. Even though the Jazz had picked me in the second round two years before in the draft, I had a mark and some of the veterans said they didn't think the team needed me. They already had a stacked two-guard position. Griffith, Mannion, Anderson, Hansen, and now, Dell Curry.

Signing that year's contract was a sigh of relief for me from my financial burdens. I'd switched agents from Earl "The Pearl" Monroe a while back to take my chances with Joe Glass as The Pearl was too busy with his company, Pretty Pearl Records. Joe was a stand-up guy and a good financial advisor. He was on it. Pearl and Alan Herman, my old agents, would stop by the house every once in a while, but Joe whom I rarely saw felt like family. Joe also admired my loyalty and how I was supporting my family but he also saw how it was wearing me down. My game was not growing to where I wanted it to be based on my expectations and those of everybody else. Coaches, and family, were the hurdles I told myself, still not seeing that I was my worst enemy.

It was time to leave the 'hood and Club 432 behind. Saying my goodbyes to Mama and the family, Mama couldn't wait until I got off the block and out of the 'hood. She even paid for the cab to the airport. This time around I was moving into the same complex as Bobby Hansen and now our new neighbor shooting guard Dell Curry. Curry my namesake, was a badass out of Virginia. He was well respected and had been named NCAA Player of the Year in '86. That year he married his high school sweetheart and spawned one the greatest shooters of all time in basketball history, his son Stephen Curry. I knew that Bobby, being from the inner city, most likely experienced drugs. But Curry was a stand-up guy like Karl. Dell at the time seemed to party as well. Unbeknownst to me, he was dipping and dabbing during the season with coke himself, but he obviously got a grip and went on to have a stellar career and family.

I was introduced to low coke by friends. My finances needed it. Low coke is small amounts of coke costing five to ten bucks to get you high but not break the bank. It was for the experimenters not for me, a hardcore user at this time. Things were strained and I was beginning to learn more or less, that you should not fuck up where you lay your head or make your livelihood. I broke that rule. As I said in the 80's cocaine was a sign of prestige, so I would go to parties expecting to take part in the consumption of a line or two of the real stuff with the who-is-who of partying. There were no chaperones in this fraternity and no drug testing unless you were out of control.

We were in L.A. for a Lakers vs. Jazz game. LA's Golden Tail Club was not far from Soul Train and Carolina's West Dance Hall and they were the spots. After Laker vs. Clippers games, I would be in there rubbing elbows with megastars, the likes of Jack Nicholson and Stevie Wonder, and was also in the company of some of the most beautiful cherubs in the bodies of humans. These beautiful women were throwing themselves at me. I could take my pick. Sometimes I would have relations with three women in a night. As I look back, I am not proud of my lifestyle at that time and what I became. I was not raised that way. Mama did not know and would have been appalled at the things I was doing. Every time I thought of how much I was disappointing Mama I would get down but there was always coke to lift me up again. Why were the streets winning against the values and morals she instilled in me? What was the defect in me that was threatening my dream? Why couldn't I dabble like others and keep my shit together? My basketball IQ was noticeable but my IQ had taken a leave. The emotional tug-of-war of coke and partying on my life and my game was stressful. I was determined to get my shit right. I went to stay at Karl's home to get away from it all. Karl had seen how I misjudged that alley-oop pass from Stockton and gone downhill from there so he and my Jazz brothers, Darryl Griffth, Dell Curry, and Rickey Green were questioning my home situation while I was questioning my playing time. We were like Batman & Robin. Karl didn't tolerate my kind of behavior and I kept my drug use away from him. I felt it was my time to shine since I had been doing such a good job lately, especially for a player from a

Division 2 school and I was determined to give it all I had. If I could lasso this thing I really had a chance to continue to shine. I had it in me. After all, I had locked down a player like Michael Jordan.

I was selected on the second defensive team in the N.B.A., meaning that I was seen as one of the top ten defensive players in the league. Sharing minutes with D. Griffith, B. Hanson, and D. Curry in the Jordan era, I was one of them holding Jordan to twenty points. That plus wins at home was the last instance that broke my silence and frustration about my playing time which dwindled yearly and in my mind was a long overdue conversation. That wasn't my only frustration, there was my family's increasing demands. I couldn't relax because I was getting calls from my family in need of help. They called for every little thing and wanted me to give them money. I was trying to focus on my career. Joe wanted to talk to my family, but I felt because he was White, well Jewish, he wouldn't understand the struggle. He said I wasn't the only family he had dealt with like mine. For many players, they became the gravy train for everyone they ever knew. So, I allowed him to have a relationship with them when I got tired of the talk going around about why my Mama was still living in 340 Clifton Place when her son was playing in the league. I withdrew every dime I had and gave it to Mama.

Distributing my contract money was not enough to help everybody. That year, it came down to me realizing I just couldn't do it as I was spending about $6,000 every day on my lifestyle of gators, linen, jewelry, and women and my designer drugs. After that, I decided to be selfish for once in my life and I stopped calling home.

Missing my 'hood, I drove the thirty-five-mile ride to Ogden, Utah to get some ghetto love. I found my real connect, the pusher man Romero, a Spanish Jazz floor photographer, and made the deal for my season tickets worth five grand for home games. Sniffing the whole ride there and back, I stopped off to meet Charles, who lived at Hale Air Force Base in Layton, Utah. I frequently went to the NCO Club with Charles, as it was a place for the corps of non-commissioned officers to have camaraderie and blow off steam. The NCO Club was where I met Kim Butler. Even though she was beautiful, I knew I didn't want to be with a woman in the military because they could get shipped out at any point. However, I was attracted to her and we exchanged numbers. Her area code was from the slums of Ogden. Isn't every slum where the army and police fore go to recruit? That night, I requested to drive her home knowing she took a bus from Ogden to Layden, Utah a few miles from her home. For me, that was a sign of a gentleman. That got me to first base with her…and I found out she was a civilian, not in the military! On the way to her house, the chemistry was mutual as both of us coming from poverty understood each other. Everything went well as far as the trust goes and I won a second date. I memorized how to find my way out to her home on my own, without Charles. Charles had been the one to show me the Black neighborhood in Ogden.

Meeting Kim's mother, Lucy, was something out of a 'hood novel. Lucy was known in the underworld and to the criminal justice system. She had the attitude of a Ma Barker and a scar on her left cheek. Her beauty was apparent but fading from the wear and tear of the streets. Lucy took us to the infamous Legion Club and she dressed like she wanted to look like the madame of the underworld. Showing me off as a trophy, I got the key to the underground city, more a tunnel being with Lucy. She scored some coke for me, but I wanted to meet Mr. B, the Ogden big Kahuna connect. I felt immortal making trips daily after practice or home games to the underworld.

Mr. B was living right under my nose the whole. time. I thought maybe this was where Romero, the photographer, was copping but I finally met him upon his request to feel me out himself after hearing about the amount I was spending on the white girl—coke. He wanted to make sure I was not sting and was a legit client. I would use a different car from Larry A. Miller's car lot to run my game than my usual. Weeks later, one of the cars I was known to drive was spotted in the 'hood. I'd let a known informant use the car, the sports photographer on the court from whom I was getting a few grams. Karl told me they were watching me. That the people in my circle, and my car were in an ongoing investigation. The law started tapping my phone. Bobby Hansen, a White player, got wind of this from an inside source and threatened me. He made it clear that if I told anyone about his involvement with drugs, he would have me killed. He stayed close enough to monitor my association before totally cutting me off.

The pressure was so great and it was coming from all around, family, coaches, players, and dealers but it all went away with every sniff of coke or sip of alcohol. Or a mixture of both. I was depressed and paranoid. I was in such a dark place, I couldn't see a shard of light. Enveloped in darkness I thought of only one way out. Doris, my rock back in New York didn't want to have anything to do with me but I still loved her and Kaleef. I couldn't even reach out to my number-one supporter of all time, Mama. There I was high as a kite, battalions marching in my head demanding more and more with a .380 pistol cocked and ready. I had purchased it when I first moved to Woodbine Condos and while on and off contemplating offing myself. Yes, I was on the verge of committing suicide but thinking about my young family and Mama, I couldn't do it. Thank God for that!

The '89 season road trip to the East was the straw that broke the camel's back. The Indiana Pacers were the first stop, then it was Philadelphia, the Nets, and Boston before the New York Knicks game. At the morning shoot-around, the pre-game warm-up, the NBA officials called me in. They had received an anonymous tip that, "Scurry was using drugs." That would be a death knell if proven and I don't think it was too hard to prove since I'd been wiretapped and watched. I went home to Clifton Place to get away from it all. Concerned about my mental state, Karl, Thurl, and Rickey had to see for themselves what my situation was. I had tried to keep my using it a secret. They were also concerned about how I could blow so much money in three days, so they came by 340 Clifton Place. Not letting me out of their sight that night was a night to remember.

Hearing of a trade after the game and learning the Knicks were bidding for my release, I was excited but wary. The deadline was over the next day. My impatience got the best of me, and I settled for the release and waiver pick-up process. That was it; my history as a Jazzman had come to an end, only to be picked up finally by my hometown the Knicks. With a quarter of a million dollars remaining on the contract with Utah, the Knicks contract could only sign me after being waived, not cut. A cut would have gotten me a whole new contract which would have given the Jazz a future draft salary cap. A salary cap is the limit, the total amount of money that the National Basketball Association teams are allowed to pay their players. The majority of the American sports leagues (NFL, NHL, MLS) have some kind of salary cap. In my case, if the Jazz got rid of me, it would lower the amount they would have to pay any other player.

Catching up to the Knicks' next game against the Spurs in San Antonio, I received a new jersey with a new number: #20. Twenty numbers have haunted me throughout my career and it felt ominous. First, at Utah Jazz, I got the number twenty-two, a number worn by John Drew, now an addict. The last I heard, he was homeless. The Knicks' Ray Richardson, who wore #20, was blackballed for life. I needed to turn the tide of the number 20! I signed two ten-day contracts that only lasted for the remainder of the season. Weeks before entering the playoffs, I sat on the bench thinking, "Shouldn't I have complained in Utah to Jazz Coach Layden about playing time earlier?" The Jazz waiving me and the Kinks picking me up, was long overdue in my opinion. I was still getting acclimated to Pitino's system which he brought over to the Knicks from his days as a college coach at Providence, Kentucky, and Louisville.

I began wondering if I would be deadweight while riding the bench. We were only five games away from hosting the Philly 76ers at home, which would be my first home game as a Knick. We would practice at SUNY College. It was every basketball kid's dream, especially a kid from Bed-Stuy to play Madison Square Garden as a Knicks. At last! Smelling the aroma, standing at the center court doing a 360, and taking in the arena felt like I was dreaming, only to be awakened by the ball boy asking me if I wanted a ball to warm up. I had to establish my existence right away to preserve a spot for the upcoming season for a new longer contract. I may have hung up my Jazz jersey as an unsung hero but I was ready to make my mark with the Knicks. This was the crucible. My first block as a Knick was against Albert King and it resulted in a fast break. I was hoping Mark Jackson understood the tapping of my right thigh that Stockon and I perfected in the Salt Lake as a signal for an alley-oop but not a chance. The ball went to good ol' Gerald Wilkens, who took off for glory.

Rick Pitino would promise me I would be back next season as a Knick. After discussing my future with the Knicks, they also had discussions with Louis Orr, Trent Tucker, Gerald Wilkens, Johnny Newman, and Kenny Walker. Why did Coach Pitino want me that badly when the bench was loaded? My chance of a lifetime I should have left well enough alone, especially after that interaction with the NBA officials.

Getting a ride from the Newark Airport in 1988 with small forward player, Kenny 'Sky' Walker, we started talking about our future as Knicks players before the conversation shifted. The next thing I know we were smoking that good 'ole Mary Jane. I'm not sure if word got back but it was 1988, shortly after that day, the Knicks decided to let me go. I was deadweight going into the playoffs. There was a rumor going around that I was a bad investment. But it wasn't a rumor…it was the truth. I blew the opportunity with the Knicks.

I had a bad image for the team because of bad moral turpitude, and my continuing and growing negative off-the-court behavior…drugs, women, partying was only too obvious. My image was tarnished.

Despite my bad behavior at home, I was still considered a great player elsewhere and was offered a deal with the Olympiacos B.C. The Greek team, referred to as Olympiacos, was based in Piraeus and it was part of the major multi-sports club, Olympiacos CFP. I took a deal worth $200,000 in Greece for the season that had just begun. I was disappointed in myself for blowing such a major opportunity with the Knicks to become one of the greats but I only had myself to blame. It wasn't my game but my life that had put up huge boulders in my path. Now, I was waiting for a call from my agent trying to hear any news before I left the States. Stupidly, I was wondering if teams were considering me a troublemaker or just an overall problem. Was I a distraction to Joe's other clients? And did Joe Glass still want to represent me after I had mismanaged my finances and was personally out of control? Well, Joe had turned my finances over to my family and they had the responsibility and they were unwittingly giving me money that I used for drugs. I had so many questions left unanswered with such little time to figure them out. However, with all of the questions floating around, I did not have the capacity to realize that the answers should have focused on one thing: my drug use. Drugs were the problem…I was the problem.

— TEN —

EUROPE

I didn't stick around for an answer to the questions I asked. I was out. I was going to Greece for the remainder of the NBA Season. Let me just say, Greece was the bombdiggity. The beautiful country on the Aegean Sea was a far cry from what I knew at home. Old, with an enviable history, though classified as Europe seemed at times like a throwback. It was welcoming and the people were warm and friendly. I couldn't believe a world outside of the US existed in such majesty.

Settling in Europe, I felt a sense of relief being away from home. This was my chance to get it right once and for all and come back home strong. Whatever drive determination and discipline I had left in me I was going to find it. The place had a heart for its people unlike the America I knew where things were more important than people. I was treated like a king. I lived in Athens surrounded by ancient history and I was a new man. Looking at the Acropolis with a history dating back some 3,000 years made me appreciate just how young my own country was in the scheme of things and that there were other realities in far-off places. The Mediterranean food was so different and savory and was far healthier than the Church's or Kentucky Fried Chicken dotting every corner in the 'hood. I was out of the toxic environment of America and I was starting afresh. I started the slow process of rehabilitation because I wanted to take back control of my life and I was feeling great.

I was given the #10 on my jersey, thank goodness, and a five-bedroom beach-front mini-mansion in a prestigious Southern town called Glyfada. This was living in a way I had not dreamed possible even in America with all my money. It was the antithesis of my life in the 'hood and people seemed so human. I could now appreciate why all those Black artists like James Baldwin and Josephine Baker made their lives abroad. I even bought myself a Yorkie I named Jazz. I experienced standing ovations as I entered restaurants after scoring 40-50 point games per night. I had returned to a game where it was pure passion and unadulterated fun. Things were different here. Winning was more rewarding and I was thriving. The European coaches were not one-sided, nor was it a "Do it my way or the highway" attitude. They respected and honored me as a player and a man. My skills were revered. I felt committed to the team and worked hard. With exposure to this different European culture with teams from across different countries, coming to play, I could clearly see how America's excessive greed being an integral part of the game made it a hostile environment for players like me. Europe was more concerned about my human needs while in the NBA league, I was just like a mule grinding a wheel. When the mule was all done, he was laid out to pasture. Others who might have had a different upbringing and influences with not as many holes in their psyche could withstand a lot more pressure than I, always living in doubt and fearing failure. The NBA's all-consuming monopolization of the talent in a dog-eat-dog world was toxic. With this more relaxed atmosphere and a whole lot less pressure, I was able to manage my impulses to use.

My life was returning and for the first time, I understood that not everywhere was America. I wanted to share this discovery with my family. While it was still business and survival back home, I wanted Mama to see I was not a lost cause and experience a new perspective besides the good old USA. Spelling my name in Greek as EAPI-XEAPI, I invited my family to experience life across the globe. I wanted to show my brothers what we gained as the Scurry Brothers. They turned down the offers.

As the best player throughout the season and possibly the best in Europe, I began to pursue the luxuries which led me back to the nightlife. Nightlife everywhere comes with the darkness of the night. I was again learning that you can take the kid out of the ghetto but you can't take the ghetto mentality out of the kid. The more notoriety I got the more I sought out "my type." I even learned the Greek language to indulge myself in the European underworld. *Scarface,* starring Al Pacino as a kingpin drug lord, was a 1983 Crime/Thriller centering around the violent drug trade and his own drug-fueled paranoia. People I hung out with in the underworld mimicked Al Pacino's role as Tony Montana in *Scarface*. In that world, I discovered hashish, which now overshadowed my drug of choice, coke. The hash was readily available and the high was mellow. I embraced it and the jet-set lifestyle that went along with it. I was a celebrity and being Black made me exotic. I did not detect any racism at the time and the people loved me, not just my basketball fans at games but the Greek people on the street and jetsetters from all over Europe. These were rich, fashionable people traveling at their every whim for unbridled pleasure. They put me on the highest pedestal. Money flowed, drugs flowed. I felt on top of the world.

I was matched up in a game against Greece's best player Nick Galis, aka Nicos Galis. Who had attended Notre Dame, and was now the leading scorer in his home country. In my match against him, I won. It put me in a favorable standing with Greek elite players. Things were going great until I dislocated my elbow. This great opportunity for me just fell apart. It looked like any possible chance of returning to the league for the rest of the season was over. I'd popped my elbow back in place to finish the game but I was not invincible. I was trying to play through it for the rest of the season but it was no use. I was shooting air balls because my arm couldn't extend to its fullest. I had to seek professional medical help for my injury and an opinion about my future as a player, period. Making my own decision I headed back to New York to get a realistic opinion. Some of the best sports medicine people were in America, period. Regrettably, I had to leave my mini-mansion, my Yorkie, Jazz, and half of my contract still owed to me. A great season would have helped me build confidence and ready me to go back home. If I had only….

Returning home I had the spoils of any player in the NBA, attitude, money, and fine clothes doused with expensive cologne so I feared no extortion or harm to my family because of my financial status. That was just the way it rolled in the 'hood. Money gets respect. At that time, many ruthless gangsters controlled Brooklyn: The original Kelvin "50 Cent" Martin, Sug, a big drug dealer, Monster Steve, T-Rock, Casino Mike, Redbug, and Bo were the headmen in charge. I wanted them to know I was still a Scurry so I would kick it with them at Ike & Regina's Club on Dekalb Ave, showing love the Brooklyn way. I felt above the law riding through the 'hood, running red lights, no worries. NA Rock, as we called it or Nostrand Avenue, was home and I didn't know yet that I was my worst enemy. Some people would pull my coattail but to avoid any altercations, I would ignore it. I was also juggling the attention of two women who believed I worked construction and recovering from an injury until the attention I was getting drew suspicion about my lifestyle. They got caught in my web of deception. Instead of proving my prowess and believing in Rick Pitino's promise of, "Returning to the '91-'92 season with the Knicks," now injured I felt I needed drugs to bring me back from the disappointment that had become my life. In my drug-addled mind, I just could not catch a break. I returned to using and did not limit my unconscionable off-court behavior: partying, drugs, and women. My agent called and told me I had to return to Greece for the remainder of my contract which amounted to $100,000. I thought I had left on bad terms because I had made my own decision to leave but they wanted me back and they had bigger things to worry about. The team's owner, George Koskotas was being investigated for embezzlement of Greek monies in their bank well worth millions and millions of dollars.

The team manager, Russo, took over Olympiacos management. He promised I would get the rest of my money and insisted they really needed me for the playoffs. It was a good getaway, besides, there were rumors that could have cost me my life going around if I stayed home. Many were talking about my negative behavior which needed a correction. Mama asked me to go back to Greece and stay there. It would be worth giving it a shot to play a few more years since a return to the NBA seemed so distant.

I didn't do any work on my elbow when I was back in the States and it was still out of alignment so I was shooting air balls when I got back. Still, I was at the peak of my career becoming great so I began to medicate the physical pain with Oxycodone that I got under the table. Oxycodone back then was touted as the miracle drug of all pain meds. Soon after, I was using the sedative effects of Oxy to dull my emotional pain as well. Highly addictive, known only by pharmaceuticals, the legal pusher men, but denied to doctors and lay people, Oxy went on to cause the death of 645,000 people by 2021. Used with other illicit substances it can cause serious side effects most often death.

When my contract was up with the Olympiacos, I took jobs in various countries. Instead of rehab, I wanted to take shots of morphine for my injuries to numb the pain for the moment but it was known to form a lifetime habitual addiction. I drew the line there. Moving on to a France league, my contracts became yearly with no option of return. Keeping up with my scoring to renegotiate, but not responding to a mandatory drug test by FIBA, slipping out the back door to somehow clean my system out with the help of vinegar to no avail, landed me in big trouble with FIBA. The doping federation requested my immediate departure from the Paris League. I began bouncing around. Being released again, so as not to return home, I took a partial contract in Brussels, Belgium. It was a very cold climate. In Belgium, they tried bringing out what was left of my greatness. Compensating me for the meager tiny 6' X 9' apartment and not the greatest salary, they gave me a 500 SL gold-colored Mercedes Benz, which proved not the best idea. But wherever you go, there you are. I couldn't catch a break or should I say I didn't give myself the opportunity to catch a break.

My season ended with another incident in Belgium. I drove drunk doing donuts in the snow and lost control of the car. I bailed out, leaving the Benz sliding down an embankment. Police tracked it back to the team's owner. They showed up at my apartment, thinking something happened to me with deep concern. They found me sprawled across the bed wreaking of alcohol. I was under arrest for damaging other cars that night. I wanted to escape my plight. After landing in a Belgium prison and being released on my own recognizance I now had a reputation too in Europe.

In disguise without the team's knowledge and before further punishment, I took a flight, the Red Eye, to LaGuardia Airport that arrived at 10:00 a.m. Flagging down a black pearl taxicab; I called an old girlfriend, Sandy, whom I had met at a club but was no longer close to, asking if I could stay at her place. I was too embarrassed to go home and needed to hide from the real problem…me. Sandy always had a thing for me so I got a pass. Any reason was good enough to give her. My only possessions were thirty days of dirty clothes and the remaining $150 I had with me. We lived with her mother, sister, brother, and her 9-year-old son, Damaris. Sandy was a good person who worked odd jobs at hotels to support herself in that small room. She was a homebody and well-grounded like Doris which I liked.

I stayed with her for about three years. I'd gone from sleeping in a five-bedroom home in Greece and having a Benz in Belgium to being in a cramped one-room house and walking everywhere or taking subway rides. My son with Doris was on my mind, but I dared not show up to her. Doris and I never married but she was still on my mind.

The women of my choice in other countries were of a different breed and they would not understand my plight. American women knew men's desires, as opposed to questioning their authority. It was good to be back home kicking it with a Sistah. Although European women catered to my every need and never complained because I was living the highlife, I felt more comfortable with the women from my same culture in the 'hood.

Eventually, this arrangement brought me two daughters, Kayla, and Dayna. Sandy and I had decided to get married because she'd become pregnant but that didn't happen for three years. I decided to commit to marrying her vowing to myself never to leave any of my children again after abandoning my firstborn son and my high school sweetheart, Doris. My son with Doris was now four or five years old and I knew he needed a role model but showing up for him in my condition was not an option. I even hid my carryings-on from Sandy who was persistent in trying to bring me back to who I used to be. When I was cutting up, she was patient.

After three years, it was time to resurface. Upon visiting Mama, I pretended I had been away all this time. I had a warm welcome from my family gathering around to hear about my adventures overseas. How odd, no souvenirs or splurging on my niece's shopping sprees, I'm sure they thought it but no one said anything. I went back home to good old Bed Stuy. Trying to rebound from three disasters, I wanted to avoid the reality or the perception of a player with no contract in sight. Having little money and wanting to hold onto my lifestyle I postured. I could do anything I wanted with my Baby Mama, she loved me that much. I kept her in the back of my mind but continued to indulge in bad behavior until crack came on the scene.

I stopped rehabilitation for my arm thinking my life was over. I was too deep in my self-pity and sorrow so I started hanging out in Club 432 on Nostrand Avenue again. I fell back in love with cocaine. I also found out that such a small amount of money and drugs could buy the company of women. I paid for a private curtained-off area in the back of Club 432; I still had about $100,000 for my contract with the Olympiakos team in Greece. I was introduced by two women to a menage-a-trois. I didn't participate I just watched the women in action. My morality was nonexistent. I was in the belly of the beast and this was the first time I ever saw two women devouring each other. I didn't want to seem like I was supporting same-gender sex, a taboo in the 'hood, so I justified it by calling it innocent enjoyment to myself. Besides, they didn't look twisted like the ones in the movie, *New Jack City*.

I started to send people to cop drugs. I started playing with the women's weaknesses by being deceptive. This was going on from '91-'94 while I was going back and forth to Europe. After a few short stints in Belgium, Venezuela, Brazil, Argentina, Chile, and Peru, I was embarrassed to take a drug test knowing my urine was tainted and I would never pass. I failed once again. I went to hang out in Paris with Milt Wagner. Milt was a player turned coach from Louisville. We decided to go to the infamous Club Bain-Douche. An old bathhouse for high-class homosexuals turned exclusive club was the happening spot to turn up the party dial that celebrityhood seemed to need. It was a favorite spot for people in fashion but many celebrities and creatives visited. On any given night you could run into people like Jean-Michel Basquiat, Yves Saint Laurent, Mick Jagger, Johnny Depp, Karl Lagerfeld, Kate Moss, and even Prince once played there. That night we ran into Spike Lee. He was there with a business associate doing business and having a drink. Spike had been one of the people cheering me on in my L.I.U. days and I wanted to acknowledge him. I was at the end of my rope from so many failures and I was high out of my mind and there was no mistaking it. In response, Spike nodded and continued with his meeting. I thought for old time's sake he would have been friendlier and I felt hurt. That night I disgraced myself before a die-hard Brooklynite who had supported me at L.I.U. Spike was probably in Paris to help him take his career back in the States to another level, while mine was spiraling rapidly downward because of my out-of-control behavior.

I had to be completely out of my mind to do the things I did high that I wouldn't do if I were sober. "Think about it," I had nice cribs, in different states and countries, a 2-car garage, the carpet wall to wall, 1000% Egyptian silk and satin sheets, and the women to go with it. There would be different women already in the hotel at most of our away games and they didn't just happen to be there. We would party like there was no tomorrow. Trust and believe, it wasn't simply because these women only wanted drugs. They were using the three-letter-word SEX as a way of life and they got paid. I had a different exotic chick every night. Some were special, like really special. How often do you meet someone that can suck a golf ball through a garden hose or can suck a dime from a parking meter? As I said, some of these women were special.

I started loving the fact that a chick could make my toes curl – wouldn't you? They had perfect bodies although most of them were fake. I could go on forever telling you all the good shit I truly enjoyed from all of this insanity. I have to admit, I was married at the time so there is no glory for any of the mindless and uncaring things I did. All I wanted to do was party and once I indulged in the crack life, things were no longer the same. I felt so free and surreal, I wanted to feel this way forever so I began a never-ending journey. The chase had begun! It takes some addicts their whole lifetime before they realize it's an endless cycle of destruction. Some die before they ever come to realize this truth.

I went back home and resumed my crazy behavior. After creeping into the house early one morning, I found a note of a possible contract for a reserve player for five months in Spain. It was a great relief and I accepted. My agent Joe sent me my reservation and I was heading to Barcelona, Spain. As much as I'd worked with Joe over the years, I had only seen him once in person when I went to his house in Long Island. However, we spoke on the phone all the time so he couldn't imagine the severity of my drug use. It's unlikely that he was not aware of my drug use as everyone in the NBA knew. When I had to see him for some reason, I put two or three sweaters on so I would look robust. Because of my drug use, I was skinny as a rail.

I got myself in better shape. I knew I had it in me. I was battling the insidious psychological battering of the ghetto, despite Mama's love and care. Why was I and so many ghetto kids prone to showing off when they think they have attained even a modicum of status? Away from the pressures of having to be THE MAN, in Spain, everything like in Greece seemed new again. My purposeful direction in life broke through the fog of drugs and before leaving I got Mama's blessing. I desperately wanted to emerge from my darkness and put all the fear, shame, self-loathing, and guilt I felt about my failure behind me. I wanted to be a man who came from greatness despite the trials of being born Black in America. I wanted to remember the 120 Lessons I'd proudly memorized.

Less than two decades removed from the civil rights movement, my psyche had been well-seeded in self-hatred. My brother, Paul, had a book covered with dust on the dresser. He too must have reached a point of reckoning or he might have gotten it from the brothers of the Black nationalist organization, The Nation of Islam who stood at the corner handing out literature. Headed by Elijah Muhammad and seceded by Louis Farrakhan in 1981, the Islamic faith had been what turned Brother Malcolm around from his hood life. I knew about the faith from the brothers on the corner handing out pamphlets. In fact, my declaration of not eating pork that had earned me a slap in the mouth was because of them. For some reason, I blew the dust off that book and picked it up. It felt light. It was titled, *Al-Qur'an*. I began to read the opening chapter, Al-Fatiha which is a prayer for guidance and mercy. Something came over me. I felt a feeling of humility. I felt my soul asking for guidance and mercy. I took the book with me on the plane and I began to study it from the moment we took off at JFK Airport. At that time, I began learning about the Muslim faith in earnest but it would take another experience to solidify my faith as a Muslim.

Right off the plane, I was rushed to the team practice. "One week away from an important game that would determine a deadlock spot in the playoff, they needed to see my skills. I would have to match up with one of the NBA's top players, George "Iceman" Gervin. George was a Detroit, Michigan man who had earned the name "Iceman" when he played pro for the Virginia Squires. He was known to be cool, calm, and collected but cold-blooded. I thought maybe the league had heard about my fiasco in Paris, France so I was nervous until I signed and sealed a deal worth $50,000 for five months. It was not much but not bad for a washed-up ex-NBA player on his last leg who had been to the welfare department at 500 Dekalb Avenue in Brooklyn before he got this cash contract.

After receiving half payment, we dropped my luggage off in a remote area of a town called Granollers, which was twenty minutes away from the center of Barcelona where city life was. The team was called Grupoifa. Back then Granollers had no nightlife and it was hard to even find a decent place to eat. After such a long trip, I didn't have enough strength for a full practice. As I settled in, I started to read my new book which took my mind off of my hunger. Besides, I still had a residue of cocaine from the days before in my system, so my appetite was null and void. I was furnished with a luxury car, and a one-bedroom apartment, the size of a loft in lower Manhattan. I would read *the Qur'an* daily.

Reading *the Qur'an* reminded me of a dude who at times visited a teammate of mine, back when I played for L.I.U. named Jeff Merriwether. His nickname was Idris, and I did not know he was into the book at that time. I liked his character. We had casual conversations about life and how it shouldn't be complicated. Sometimes I'd zone out and not pay attention when he was speaking, but in many ways, those conversations answered questions and feelings I had developed through the years as a God body or Christian. Idris seemed more put together than the rest of us.

To avoid the cravings of my addiction, morning practice was where I met the rest of the team to work off the yen. It was also where I would meet the president and local owners for any money transaction I needed for my yet-to-be wife and children back home. I wired money so Sandy could get a new home away from her mother's apartment. By that time, I had abandoned Doris and my son Khaleef and did not support them. Focusing on my game, I felt word would get back to the NBA League about my comeback.

GAME NIGHT. I ended up with 40 points and a thunderous alley-oop dunk that ended the game. As the MVP, "The Iceman" used to shell out 42 points, this was his first loss since his arrival when the season first started months before. Even lame I was a stallion, not yet ready to be put out to pasture. It was a reason to celebrate. I didn't want to go home alone with such a victory on a Saturday night. Befriending a local club owner named Carlito who spoke very good English, I found myself again in the presence of alcohol. I was glad Carlito spoke English because despite using the same alphabet as English, I found speaking Spanish was very different from speaking Greek and this was not the Spanglish I spoke in Washington Heights. This was Castilian Spanish and I was at a loss. The only communication I had so far was with a teammate with whom I found a connection to get weed and weed only, so Carlito was a nice addition to my Rolodex.

It seemed everybody in Spain expected people from the U.S. to be party animals. Women can be distracting and I needed a distraction from using. Hearing the women of Spain were sexual teasers, I found them a diversion. I shifted my addiction needs. I met Carmen, then Maria Jose. She was a beautiful brunette with blue eyes, 5'5", and looked like Demi Moore. I had her as my Spanish wife and she was a lookout when going to Carlito's Club where she introduced me to my first score of coke since my arrival in the back room of the club. The *Qu'ran* slowed me down but it didn't fully quell my first love. Carlito was off-limits to the average customer. The red carpet treatment brought me back to the times at Club 432 in Brooklyn. It was "mug night" and the glasses were the size of miniature kegs filled with champagne. I had a secret compartment of coke in the lining of my pants. I had once again found the party scene. At 1:00 a.m., when the town of Granollers closed down, everybody was headed to Barcelona's red light district. I was trying not to get caught up in a *Midnight Express* scenario like the star of the movie trafficking drugs across the border while I was so far from home, so Barcelona was the spot.

I was heading out on my own with a GPS pointing to a club called PARATI. Securing any detection of coke from police dogs, I sniffed the last of it; I checked my rearview mirror for signs of powder on my nose. Playing my favorite songs of Eric B & Rakim, Mary J. Blige, and Kenny G, at last, I pulled into VIP parking, feeling a sense of home. I opened up with gin and juice, a drink I learned from Greece that would not leave me with a hangover. Coming down off the coke high I needed more alcohol to lift me up. For the ride back to Granollers, Carlito needed a ride. This was my chance to have a designated driver which would allow me to consume more alcohol. He returned soon after finding himself in the company of a woman and told me he decided to leave with her. Upon hearing the last call for alcohol, I got ready to leave all alone. That night, I made it home without incident. But I had once again traveled to the dark side. I had found the seedy underbelly of Barcelona.

— ELEVEN —
THE CAR ACCIDENT

I'd caught my first DUI in Utah at the age of twenty-four. There was no hiding the shit because this was what showed up in the Utah paper.

> *LAYTON, Utah -- Utah Jazz reserve forward Carey Scurry was placed on one-year probation and fined $600 Friday after pleading guilty to a reduced charge of intoxication, 4th Circuit Court officials said. Scurry, 24, of New York, was arrested Aug. 9 and charged with driving under the influence, disorderly conduct, and giving false information to a police officer. In exchange for his guilty plea to the intoxication charge, Judge Roger Bean dismissed the other charges. Bean sentenced Scurry to 90 days in jail but suspended the jail term to 12 months on probation and ordered him to enroll in an alcohol rehabilitation program.*

> *'I don't think he knows enough about alcohol and the effects it has on people,' Bean said. 'We see alcohol as a pretty destructive force in the lives of many.'*
>
> *The judge also ordered the third-year NBA player to perform 32 hours of community service. Scurry will have to pay $100 of his fine to Layton City and an equal amount to Utah's victim restitution fund.*

I did not learn my lesson. I had since totaled my gold Mercedes and had driven countless times under the influence of substances and alcohol. This was the accident that would end my career for good.

In March 1994, after a life-threatening injury, I was officially unfit to play basketball ever again. This was not a basketball injury but a serious car accident while I was under the influence. Unlike when I was twenty-four, the newspapers didn't mention the severity of my injuries and I wasn't volunteering any information. I had celebrated after a triumphant big game in Barcelona with alcohol and coke. Driving in the mountains from Barcelona to Granollers on the narrow roads there was a lot of mist. To make matters worse I was continually nodding off and lost control. The car was totaled, I broke my neck, had cervical spine injuries, and was totally battered. My passenger, my coke supplier Carlito, broke his collarbone. He ran away from the accident with a broken collarbone and God knows what other injuries because he did not want to get picked up by the authorities and arrested. My life flashed before me. What a waste. I had reached my dream of being an NBA player and though I was not ready to accept it, I had single-handedly destroyed that dream. My nightmare was just beginning.

My agent informed me I had to uphold my end of the bargain from another DUI I'd caught in Utah and skipped out on. I could be arrested on an open warrant if I didn't address the case and come clean. To close my case, I had to do a 30-day program supervised by them. Their choice was John Lucas Wellness and Aftercare Program in Houston, Texas. The rehabilitation center was founded by John Lucas, a former NBA star whose career was derailed by drugs, and who knew my story, like his own, as an addict. He initially created a center to help addicted athletes and there were many but this place had professional clientele from every walk of life, doctors, lawyers, judges, actors, and athletes alike.

    Before entering the program, I was feeling somewhat whole again though I had slipped backward a little, it was nothing like when I was using in Bed Stuy. Despite knowing my career could be over, I was delusional as only a legend in his own mind playing in an elite tournament could be. The program cost $35,000. I didn't have that kind of money so John, understandably, knowing my playing and financial history helped me out. I did not have to pay the full fee.

    The first twenty-five days were brutal. I was climbing the wall craving drugs. In detox, I was anxious, tired, and sleepless well aware that I was psychologically and physically dependent on drugs. Even though I knew I couldn't keep living like I was, the thought of another hit was all-consuming. My physical symptoms left me feeling like I had been run over by a truck. My body ached, I was hot then cold. It was so challenging at the beginning, I wanted to give up but I knew had to get there. I had to become sober. This was my last chance…do or die. Night after night I went through withdrawal having unrelenting nightmares and waking up in cold sweats. I tried hard to be rational, to remind myself that drugs had taken everything from me…and I was now in a world of my own making. I wanted to find the strength to face the demons that have haunted me my whole life but I also kept thinking one more hit would make them all go away.

    Days felt endless and the torment unbearable. By the twenty-fifth day, I started to feel I might make it through and felt a flicker of hope. I was determined to get my act together regardless of the deep pain and conflicting emotions. Because of all the trouble I had caused Mama, my family, and the team, I was feeling committed. I was determined to get clean to try and erase the embarrassing moments I had perpetrated over and over again. As the fog of drugs lifted, I began to feel better about myself. I could do this for Mama, I could do this for Doris, I could do this for my children and Sandy but most importantly I could do this for me. There was a chance of redemption for a new beginning and I had, in Houston Texas, taken the first step to reclaiming my life.

Even after twenty-five days when I started to feel myself again, I knew I needed more time. John Lucas in his infinite mercy decided to extend my therapy which included workouts on the Houston Oiler's field on the campus of T.C.U. (Texas Christian University). We were under the care of Doc, a sports trainer who helped many athletes come back from failing careers. I was ready for what he dished out. I was going the extra mile at the Oiler's Stadium he'd built. On a huge man-made hill outside the gym, we ran sprints up and down. It was a minor-league atmosphere. A long battle was ahead I knew that, but I felt ready. Mentally I felt ready and physically Doc saw to it that we were in shape.

At the gym, Doc introduced me and Chris Washburn, a 6'10" power forward with a child-like mentality to consistent workouts. I was doing well and feeling strong again. Word got back to Coach Don Chaney of the Houston Rockets. He had to witness my rehabilitation for himself so he invited me to the Rockets Summer Camp and to the summer pro league in L.A., with a small starting forward position. Having an outstanding performance along with an M.V.P. Award and dropping a triple-double at summer camp won me a trip to the big dance, which in this case was veteran's camp, and he was impressed.

I was feeling alive again. My jersey #2, too was a relief…nothing in the twenties though it started with a 2! Things could be looking up. The jersey had my name written all over it. Man, I was feeling proud and alive and I was ready to show the world just who Carey Scurry could be once and for all. I was no washed-up, broken-down jock…I was in this for the win which could at last be coming through. Before the invitation to the '94-'95 season and when the roster of players for that year was to be finalized, news reached Coach Chaney that I had had an accident that left me with a neck injury. Calling me out of the last luncheon at summer camp, he told me that the chance of future injuries was too risky. They saw me as a bad investment. This was the final blow. I was released and it was the Rocket's decision. There I was, an opportunity to play again alongside NBA greats, Hakeem Olajuwon, Kenny Smith, Otis Thorpe, Rodney McCray, and a contract worth millions watching my life once again evaporate. I watched my dream go right back down the drain. What was the purpose of this life? What was I here to learn?

After that, I felt emotionally, financially, and spiritually bankrupt and the old response was kicking in, to use mainly to escape. I turned to my faith for guidance and mercy. *Al-Qur'an* categorically states that intoxicants and gambling are specifically forbidden…in modern interpretation, which means drugs. I didn't want to hear that and even as I pretended to be of the Nation of Islam, and even as I read every spiritual material I could get my hands on, my feeling of self-worth was in the toilet. I wanted to forget. Deflated and disappointed, I didn't have the desire to see family any time soon. Flying back home, having the book in hand, I began to deeply explore my spiritual life. I felt it was a better way and it would steer me in the right direction. I wanted Sandy to embrace Islam. Two of us against the beast would be better, but juggling such a young, tender family and being financially strapped it was hard for her. I stuck with the religion, but I had a hard time convincing Sandy to become a serious student of the book. After that, I tried to force it on her instead of leading by example. Her resistance made me doubt my further participation in our relationship, so I began straying away from home. I was saddened by our situation but going back to my old life was not something I wanted to do.

I ran into an old player, Malik Hajj. He saw the stress on my face and told me to follow him into a building on 4th Avenue in downtown Brooklyn. It was Al-Farooq Majid mosque. The six-story converted factory with its orange and gold trim was where Arab Brooklynites worshiped. I raised one finger reciting an oath of declaration (Shahada), the belief that there is only one true and living God and no other and that Muhammad is the final and sealed messenger of God. This was a hard pill for my girlfriend to swallow since she was raised in a Christian home and so was I. I couldn't understand why it was so hard. God has had many messengers.

Still, I felt I was always disappointing and letting my family down. My belief was family first. Despite all my shortcomings, I felt responsible for taking care of them. I decided it was time to get married. But not before I went back to my old ways of hanging out until the wee hours. I would in time come to have *the Qur'an* in one hand and the pipe in the other.

But when I made a promise I kept it. I would marry Sandy who had the patience of Job. I don't know why Sandy put up with me. It was probably to have bragging rights and to say she was the chosen one of a celeb though I was hardly that anymore. One morning, I stepped out of Club 432 to fulfill that promise to Sandy. Strolling down Nostrand Avenue, I ran into Mama and my sister, Linda, who were standing on the corner of Clifton Place and Nostrand Avenue. I told them I was on my way to get married to Sandy. They didn't believe me. Since I had so many women I considered to be trophies, settling down was a far-fetched concept in their minds, but it was true. I stopped at Gentlemen's Quarter's Men's clothing store on Fulton Street to buy an outfit for the occasion and to get out of what I was wearing that smell of liquor, weed, and women from the after-hours spot.

Meeting my future wife, Sandy downtown in front of the municipal building on Joralemon Street, we had a quick ceremony. After that, handing my new bride a few bucks she and her sister Donna went off to celebrate as I left for my personal celebration with my boys from the 'hood back at Club 432. After rehab, I had tried to stop my bad habits overnight, and one of the ways to stay clean was not to return to the environment that supported my habit. But where had I to go but back to my sorry neighborhood where my sniffing cocaine was now even expected. Looking back, I was childish, foolish, and embarrassed. It is something I wish I could turn the clock back on and change.

As my life spiraled, I moved from cocaine the gentleman's drug to crack. The moment I hit the pipe I knew my life was truly over. The euphoria meant I would be back over and over again. My glory days were long over. It's funny how all those nights I spent in hotels listening to the hooray, cheers, and chanting, "Scurry, Scurry, Scurry, Carey Scurry," quickly faded away. I had been in the game long enough to know that all these inspirations and promises that began with lofty gifts and fat budgets inevitably shrink in value. I hadn't yet blamed myself for my own demise. Ashamed, I moved out of Clifton Place. As I drove further and further from the block back to the apartment I rented from Lucy, an old addict, on DeGraw Street in Park Slope, I wanted to pretend the cheers were still there. I had turned into what my Mama had said, a washed-up junkie. Still, I was trying to find the high life in Park Slope at Club 200 on Union Street. 5th Avenue was too slow for my speed and I needed to drown my sorrow for the failure of my promising life.

My wife and children, Damaris, Kayla, and Dayna, rarely saw me. I would give her a few bucks here and there but Sandy had to find odd jobs to maintain their living situation. I was so out of it, I didn't consider their feeling or welfare. I was living an unconscionable and delusional life! Because I was the NBA player, Carey Scurry,

I felt I was above the law which was so far from the truth. After ten years of marriage, I finally divorced Sandy and married the crack pipe. I had hit rock bottom and was running around the 'hood like a chicken with its head cut off. I was slapped with possession and misdemeanors. To this day, I dread and fear the law. And the worst was yet to come.

— TWELVE —
WHEN LIFE SHOWS UP

There were no more deals. Slipping in under my family's nose back to Club 432, spending what little I had on coke and women, I became a regular at the club. Nothing was off limits for me now… not even the dreaded crack. From daybreak to the after-parties of a trap (crack) house, my life became a complete train wreck. Loaning my car out for drug favors, and not being able to pay my debts, I was mistakenly accused of heisting a drug package that was missing. Being sought after for theft, ducking, and dodging, I ended up cornered, stripped of my clothes, threatened to be thrown off a roof, and begging for grace time and time again. I couldn't fathom how the fuck I'd gotten here! My drug use antics should have killed me a few times over but it was doing nothing to take me out of my misery. I should have offed myself because this was the limit. How had I failed this miserably? I had squandered millions of dollars over my career and here I was back where I started butt naked hanging upside down over a roof. It was 2006 and I had been using it for twenty years.

Since 1965, NBA players vested in the league for over three years get a monthly pension. Back in my time, it was $559 per month per year of service along with benefits such as health care and college tuition programs. My $ 1,677-a-month NBA check was late, and knowing I had run out of money and rent was due, I asked Mama for some help from the money I had given her over the years before. The money I gave her was hers to do as she pleased. Mama did not give me any money but she did help Sandy and our children financially.

Now I was doing whatever it took to get drugs when my money ran out. I would heist stuff from people and even steal from Mama. The moment my check came I used it to get high. I couldn't face reality.

Money started getting very low, so low that I had to start busting moves if I wanted to keep on smoking. That's right, I had run out of money. My NBA checks weren't coming fast enough so now I had to do what I had to do, and that's when the game changed. I started doing stupid shit such as boosting. Yes, I was stealing whatever I could from wherever I could, including Mama. I was like the crackhead Samuel L. Jackson played in Spike Lee's movie, *Jungle Fever*. Whatever it took to get this money so I could continue to buy more drugs, I did. I was so far gone; I didn't care who knew at this point. I was 188 pounds, when I went to the NBA I was now a scrawny, bedraggled vagrant.

Once I went off the deep end, I was finished. I couldn't fool anybody; I didn't want to do anything else in life except smoke crack 24-7 instead of going to get help. Hell no, I wanted to smoke even if it meant smoking in a crack den apartment where the only lights were candles, infested with bedbugs, and rats the size of cats. We thought it would be funny to put a collar on them and take the rats for a walk on the street. Writing about it now seems surreal and makes the hair stand on the back of my neck. I'd pluck a bedbug that was biting the shit out of me off and keep smoking like it was nothing. Then I'd take a cigarette lighter and burn it until it popped. I am sure you're thinking at that point I should have just left this den of evil.

Wrong! I just went to another room. Big difference. It was like changing seats on the Titanic, a sinking ship. The weather determined where I smoked, which was mostly indoors in winter. Of course, in wintertime, I wanted to be inside for obvious reasons. It's very hard to flick a lighter when your fingers are cold. I always wanted to be inside if I could find someplace where the heat was turned on. Of course, summer days were better because I could smoke anywhere in the hallways, roofs, basements, and even openly in the street. God knows I wanted to stop. I just couldn't. The crack wouldn't let me stop, not to mention those who I used it with. I was also using other substances. Drugs wanted and demanded more and more from me. Because I had been an NBA basketball player, I was given a lot of chances to change my life and do the right thing.

The chance of a lifetime eluded me because it meant I would have to make vital decisions only I could make, to change the people, the places, and the things that were bad influences. I failed to make those decisions, instead turning to a life of crime, and to total, what now seemed irreversible, substance abuse. All I had to look forward to now was death. Falling in love with the drug game almost cost me my life again. I sniffed heroin like it was coke, passing stems around from people known to have H.I.V., having unprotected sex not knowing my partner's medical history. I was exposed to all kinds of rat-infested apartments where buckets were used as bathrooms. I began to doubt if those around me even cared because if they did, they would have tried to stop me or at least convinced me that wearing the same clothes day after day was not alright.

Crack had me believing that everything I did was okay but I was not okay. Not to mention, I was losing weight by the second, so I'd put on 2 or 3 sweaters to keep from looking like a scarecrow. Mama and the rest of my family tried everything to get me straight…threats, intervention, you name it. They were devastated. Their efforts were useless and their pleas fell on deaf ears. So, doing what I thought was best, I convinced myself to take another hit.

Since my release from my first prison sentence, I had slept in the corridors of Louis Armstrong Housing Projects and taken chances while the N.Y.P.D. was shooting residents during routine patrols. I remember a young man named Terrence was killed while running roof-to-roof returning CDs for a party he was supposed to DJ. I noticed that the even more aggressive policing in Bed-Stuy came with the influx of middle-class whites and millennials moving into the community. I was scared for my life, yet on the other hand, I didn't care because I hated who I had become. I had the scruffy look of a derelict chasing a high. It was embarrassing sleeping on the roof of my Aunt Janie's apartment. She allowed me to use her bathroom to take a bath and she also fed me as I didn't dare show up to Mama in my condition. I would disappear soon after being fed and cleaned up in pursuit of my next fix. My values and morals were non-existent.

MY FIRST ARREST

Someone Snitched. Where I grew up, people stood by codes as though they were the law. In the mean streets of Brooklyn, they were indeed the law and a snitch could be in big trouble if found out. In Bed-Stuy, the code of the streets, the pledge one took was— never, ever snitch. I mean we had badass leaders, beasts, prostitutes, and many other derelicts. At the end of the food chain was the dirtbag…the snitch! A snitch is usually a street person who pledges with the police to receive a small cash payment to make a statement against someone. This statement may or may not be true. For the police, it seemed not to matter as long as they got what they needed to make an arrest.

Police call these low-level criminal snitches confidential informants or "C.I.s" because they are considered confidential and the don't have to appear in court. Only the statement they make will be used. To a jury, as I would learn, their statement carried as much weight as that of a police officer. It was worth more than anything I could ever say. The word of a drug-addicted, low-level criminal paid for by police is worth more to a jury than my life! What happened to cross-examination, innocent until proven guilty, and due process? Not for the poor, not for those who pledge themselves to the streets, no matter how innocent. Hypocrisy runs deep no matter who or what you have pledged because the streets have a way of conspicuously transforming a person no matter who you are. Today, there is no longer a loyalty code. The laws of the court have nothing to do with getting a fair trial by a jury of your peers. They are purposely designed to work for those in power like the police.

Since I had been committing petty crimes to support my habit, I became a familiar face to the surrounding precincts, 79, 88, 83, and 77. Still thinking I was above the law and getting celebrity treatment, I was acting like an airhead. Mama, finding me unbearable to deal with decided to have the 'hood take my fate into their hands. They were actually applauding as the police hauled me away, hoping it would be my redemption. People pointed at me saying, "They got Scurry." Some applauded, some laughed, and some were upset because I was their best customer.

When I entered the court the booking officers knew me well. People were rallying around like they had when I was a local celebrity. I also had a good attorney and though I'd been a nuisance, this was my first arrest. The judge was lenient and instead of jail time, I was remanded to sixteen months in rehab at a place called J-Cap. J-Cap was, and I believe still is, a drug treatment center in Saint Albans, Queens. N. Y. Everyone was hoping I could turn my life around and get a second chance to start my life over. I was accepted to J-Cap, an in-patient program. I'd been able to beat the rap somewhat.

My wife tried one last time to reassure me and give me hope by letting me know she would keep the vows of our marriage through sickness and health. That Sandy would take me back if I were clean, and since I wanted to be a good father to my children, I had high hopes of trying to do better. Was I too far gone for a comeback? In J-Cap I did a lot of reflecting on my life but I wasn't ready to take responsibility for it. Rehab was far better than jail. Feeling I'd gotten a pass once again because I was King Scurry, rather than face reality, I continued in my delusion. While at J-Cap a check came to Mama from my agent who did my taxes. It was worth $7,000. Being slick I got a pass to be escorted on a medical trip, which was only a plot I hatched to deviate to Mama's house to pick up the check. Mama handed me the check but I saw the worried look on her face that I'd do something crazy. I didn't do anything crazy. I went directly to Mr. Rand's Liquor Store on Clifton & Bedford and cashed the check. He didn't ask questions. As requested, Rand gave me half of the money which left $3,500 to pick up a later day. On my way back to J-Cap, with $3,500 in hand, well $3,450 since I gave my escort $50 hush money to drop his guilt, I called my wife and told her to go to Rands for the rest of the money. I felt relieved to be able to solve some of our problems.

In my mind recovered, and twelve months later, I left rehab. My sentence was for a sixteen-month remand. Did I last, no. My body had gotten a break and I was feeling good so I felt the additional four months weren't needed. I intended to return to my tender family, but the desire to get high returned immediately. With the money I stashed burning a hole in my pocket, I again went to the land of make-believe where drugs usually led me. There I was King Scurry once again. And as King Scurry, I had seen and done too much and had the right to forget.

JAIL THIS TIME

Twelve months in J-Cap were not enough. Naturally, my stupidity and desperation led to my first real jail conviction. At the age of forty-two, so delusional, I still wanted to go back to the league, but there I was on Gates Avenue at 8:00 a.m. and again in police custody. My body was going through withdrawals from the white cloud of crack smoke even as I stood facing twenty-one to forty-five years in front of a black-robed judge who swung his gavel announcing my case was remanded after pleading not guilty. That meant my case was sent back to the trial court where it originated. In the interim, I was to be held in custody. I was about to be on my way to Riker's Island, to await a new court date. I still had thoughts of getting high even knowing I might not see freedom or the light of day for a long time. The only thing I was willing to accept was a multi-million-dollar contract and a starting spot on a team in the NBA, not a jail sentence. My arrogance was totally way off base. Even after all these years I was still in shock about my departure from the league and seeking sympathy from the family I had abandoned. More importantly, though, right then, I needed $10,000 for bail. I was a repeat offender. There was no question I'd be given time.

    I finally called Mama, knowing she was sick from worrying about me. I knew she would be glad to hear from me and not from the morgue. I was wrong though. She had reached her limit with me and went as far as not letting me into her home and now she thought I was getting what I deserved. Desperate, I attempted to contact my father, who had been absent most of my life hoping guilt might get him to put up the bail money. He expressed his hurt knowing he had failed me. I asked for bail to no avail. I did see him at Mama's funeral when I was in my late 50s. Although we were strangers, we made peace with each other in the moment.

    I had spent the previous night smoking a little over $1,000 of crack cocaine. I was told my charges were burglary in the 2nd degree, which was a felony. I had faced charges before but never such a serious one as this offense. There I was being charged with burglarizing someone I made more money than in the NBA. I blamed my ego and addiction for my plight and the trips from crack house to crack houses sleeping on dirty couches and mattresses. There was nothing positive about it. Trying to impress the fellas, junkies to boot I ended up a sucker. I'd left my Mama in a one-room apartment and my wife and kids in a cramped two-bedroom, one-bathroom apartment on the 4th floor with the Q Train right outside our window, near Prospect Park that people used as a shelter in the summertime for the crack den. Even my conscience was gone. The Mama I loved; the Mama who sacrificed so much for her children; the Mama who had warned me against the life I was now living was watching me closing in on death. My wife and children were not a match for the vice grip drugs had over my mind and body. To lessen my guilt, I never saw my family. My family now began taking out insurance policies on my life, thinking I wasn't going to make it through another winter. The Carey Scurry name no longer held any weight like it once did. I was now just an average Joe junkie at this point and not too many people gave a flying fuck about me. I had become a regular crackhead like the rest of them.

I had been in a rehab facility now three times. What would it take for me to straighten my life up? I wondered about all this as I was sitting on the bus prison bound where I'd be until my trial since I couldn't raise the bail money. Seconds seemed like hours. I used to dread the feeling of being dead because the applause had stopped and here I was, deafening silence all around and no matter how delusional I was, there was no chance in hell of another contract coming my way. Still, my addiction and delusion were no joke. I was living out of bounds all the while still retreating into my imaginary world.

We drove through the small city of prison buildings to the OBCC building, aka O'Boy, also known as the Otis Bantum Correctional Center and named after the second Warden. It is one of eight prisons on Rikers Island and should only be a 24-hour holding center for people awaiting bed assignment. I was processed and issued a D.O.C. (Department of Corrections) cup, blanket, towel, toothbrush and Oraline toothpaste, orange Patakis slip-ons, two small bars of Corcraft soap, and an I.D. that must be worn at all times. The soap was so strong, it was like lye and irritated and discolored my skin. I realized I was not in the five-star hotels I had gotten used to in my brief heydays in the U.S. and Europe. This was the lockup, the bullpen…prison, my current cold, hard life reality.

I noticed a lot of C.Os. (Correctional Officers) who took the job route right out of high school to serve the influx of this growing criminal problem in our community. I wanted to bury my head in the ground like an ostrich. I was recognizing teammates, family, and friends who took the C.O. test and passed now on the other side of the fence.

I was then escorted by an old friend, Ty Whitehead, one of many who never looked down on me. He assigned me a bed. After making my bed, I lay down and prepared to face the music; I played the blame game over and over. Who is to blame? My Father? The Utah Jazz Coach? Racism? Poverty? The bad luck number on my jersey? I could blame just about anything and anybody but me. I thought back to when I was born. I was Cake mix, adorable with chubby kissable cheeks so what happened? I was haunted by the thought of stealing from Mama's house to support my addiction. Everyone close to me had felt my wrath and larceny. I contemplated calling Mama.

Deep down, I still felt I could walk out of this situation unscathed because I was Carey Scurry, the legend who deserved better. I thought of getting high at times but I was too frustrated with the situation. I even ran into a dealer from the 'hood who gave me some crack. I should have flushed it in the toilet rather than given it to a fellow inmate in hopes of a return favor one day. I thought to myself, where did my money go? Why didn't I save any of it? I knew I had squandered it getting high and being irresponsible. I forced myself to wake from my delusional dream world.

I thought of my wife going through all the hell I put her through dealing with my addiction. Sandy was a good person who neither did drugs nor drank alcohol so the empathy she must have had to tolerate my sickening behavior was of Mother Theresa's level. I recalled taking a portion of the kid's savings or even all of it and though Sandy was disappointed and had worked so hard to earn that money, she somehow found it in her heart to forgive me. I would then ask Mama for the money I had given her in the past. My mind then drifted to when I would leave my children alone to go buy drugs from all types of shady characters coming to our home. I totally disregarded anyone's safety if it wasn't beneficial to me. My addiction had me crying before my five-year-old and two-year-old children. They were caring little girls and would ask Daddy, "What's the matter; and why are you crying? You're going to make us cry."

I couldn't take what I was doing any more to my family and decided to leave for good and spare them my demise. I remember when I had phoned their mother to tell her I was leaving, she'd rushed home hoping I wouldn't take the kids or violate them in any way. She was probably sick of drugs falling out of my pockets or being left behind in the bathroom, and I couldn't blame her. I was also giving her mixed messages about our marriage because sex had stopped. She hung on for dear life until she decided the safety and welfare of the children were more important than her husband and our marriage. If she hadn't taken responsibility, our children would not be in our custody. My baby mama Doris, and son Kaleef, long gone, were no longer a part of my life. I had no contact with them and I am sure that's what Doris intended.

THE PLEA DEAL

I was back in the courtroom. My trial had begun. My first offer was five years which I wanted to turn down based on the victim's identification of the "perp" who was supposed to be 5'6" and 170 lbs. I stand 6'9." Look up the word 'plea' in the dictionary. In short, it means, "false reasoning, vicious reasoning, misjudgment of reasoning, a white lie, to pretend, etc." So, the judge was telling me to accept falsity for five years in prison because the police paid for a drug-addicted snitch who said I did it. My eldest daughter's advice was to take the five years. Yes, I did go J-Cap previously and now that was being used to force me to accept a five-year prison plea bargain. No one seemed on my side this time.

The jury deliberated for one hour with only one question about the difference between trespassing and burglary. Either, they had evidence for both; one was circumstantial; and the other was direct evidence. Based on my height, I should have walked. Based on the DNA, I would have a permanent home in prison.

As the jury reached its verdict, I stood emotionless, contemplating my options. There was a real battle between my feelings. The verdict on all counts was guilty, guilty, guilty. I dreaded the reality of the sentencing running consecutively on all 15 counts of burglary in the 2nd degree knowing it would consume the rest of my life. Accepting the plea deal was a hands-down decision. I had indeed committed criminal trespassing in a residential dwelling, which is burglary 2, burglary in the second degree. I needed money for drugs because my funds from the NBA, Greek, and South American teams had run out. I was foolish and thought I could get away with it. I was Mr. Invincible again. The reality of my wrongdoing hit me hard. I took the plea deal. Being humiliated in court before those who love me and the thousands who knew me from my NBA glory days was just the very beginning.

Leaving the courtroom, sitting in the back before the go-backs, which is a housing unit before permanent placement, I downplayed certain things if not disregarded them altogether. Too many feelings could get me into a whole lot of trouble. I've always known the difference between right and wrong and Mama always said there is a price I had to pay when I did wrong and I was paying that price once again. Prison was my punishment and I vowed it to be my last.

Mr. NBA, Brooklyn's finest had gone too far this time. I had never been to prison, except to see Cliff when Mama tried to scare me straight. I had long forgotten my pledge to never see a life like his. Now here I was walking down from intake to another screening post with two draft bags. It was surreal and I felt like I was staring in the movie alongside Michael Clark Duncan in *The Green Mile*. Real prison was no joke. As Cliff had said, it was survival of the fittest and worse than the streets of Bed Stuy if one could ever imagine that. Extorted, being recruited by gangs, or getting punked for other reasons was commonplace. Inmates stood by their block windows looking for those who they knew or for fresh meat to terrorize; those whose first time it was up north. As I turned into the F1 Block, I heard a familiar voice coming from the F2 Block. It was Barkin from Greene Avenue, a well-known gangster throughout Brooklyn. His classification had dropped from the maximum status and he'd been transferred to F2 Block.

I was told to report to the C.Os 'bubble,' desk station, to be assigned a bed. Being called out by my government excited me for a second and I thought, perhaps, the C.O. was a fan, only to get snapped back to the reality of me being the dorm mascot. From that moment on, I realized I was no longer a world-renowned great ballplayer anymore, no longer the fabulous Carey Scurry. I was just a number.

Unpacking in my small cube I was stationed between two felons. There was no privacy. A large safe-size locker was assigned. If you are persona non grata one is likely to find a can top in their locker. A can top, like you might find on a tuna can with sharp edges that could be used as a weapon. It's a warning to get in line with prison protocol. Next time it could be used on your neck. There was a smaller locker that doubled as a desk with a public school combination lock to which the C.O. had the master key. We all knew to have no contraband in that locker because on any given day, the C.O. who might have had a bad day with his wife could burst in and raid the locker as the outlet for his anger. The wall that stood between us was waist high allowing us to see the next man's property. This enabled sneaky thieves to exist. It, I felt sure was all a plan to have us at each other's throats. The place was a right hell hole. Grievances would get you more time in the isolation box for solitary confinement or your food tampered with.

Ulster is a little hick redneck town on the Hudson. In this small town, it seemed all the officers were related. Many inmates who were found with contraband and sharp objects got a Tier 3 or box time. It's the gravest penalty for one who commits an offense. Tier 3 can mean solitary conferment or a transfer to another more lockdown jail, shipped out with a Red ID alerting other C.Os that they're a problem. The dorms were filled with double bunks in a single cube and each held sixty inmates, After ninety days of assessment, the powers that be started calculating whether a draftee was to be transferred to another prison or maybe shipped out back to their home depending on their sentence. That's if the C.O. likes you. And C.Os in Rikers believe they own the prisoners.

Adjacent to the dorm was a room where all activity was allowed. A long way from my former life of luxury all I had access to was a microwave and hotpot which was to be used cautiously. Hopefully, you could trust that other inmates didn't put urine in the hotpot or intentionally burn out the microwave, which would leave us having to wait six months for another one. The movie room was the size of the pigeon coup I had in Williamsburg and had no ventilation. Movies were controlled by the front office. Sensing tension over TV rights, there were posted times for the different ethnic groups, mostly Hispanics and Blacks. 4:00 – 6:00 p.m. Spanish Channel 47 for the 44 Spanish brothers. Blacks wanted to watch BET after 6:00 p.m., so to avoid a race riot the signs were prominently posted.

Ten-minute showers, when there was water, were run on a timer. If you wanted more shower time you'd have to humble yourself to a twenty-year-old White C.O. to beg for another five minutes. It was like a real-life *12 Years a Slave* movie, hurrying just to get the soap out of your eyes. Showering was a challenge to have any privacy and get your business done in such a short ten-time frame. Often the C.O. didn't give a shit whether I had completed my ablutions.

We were assigned jobs for way less pay than minimum wage; it was pennies per hour. They upheld the 13th Amendment which upheld involuntary servitude for crimes. Picking up trash on the highway in orange coveralls was still a thing but prisons had graduated way past that with the advent of the Prison Industrial Complex idea. A bunch of rich people and the government realized that they could better utilize the prison population for economic gain. Big businesses were benefiting to the tune of 4 billion dollars a year from prison labor. This created a demand for more prisons to be built to expand the economic profit of these businesses. Again, minority folks were being pimped as the prison population was mostly made up of people of color.

At our facility, you were either a dorm porter or worked lawns & grounds during the winter and summer. Or, you opted to go to the prison school's Pre-GED Class, which the majority of times was closed. The only support we could look for was from a religious group or family members visiting. Most of the time, family died off or moved on so visitation was minimal. I was still struggling with my new-found faith, only to see its full effect on true believers. There were people in jail who were transforming their lives through their faith. And there were many frauds, Christians, and Muslims alike posturing. There were things I had yet to see outside the prison. Walls of rosary beads, dhikr beads, bibles, Qur'ans, and kufis, filled to the top with tithes from repenting prisoners were always there as encouragement and recidivism recognized them. Prison can do that to you. People found their faith and prison chaplains were always there to help pave the way to enlightenment.

Being selected as their Amir (Assistant Pastor), I decided to accept the responsibility only to use it as a platform for my growth and development. While giving the Khitab, otherwise known as the pulpit address, I developed more responsibility for more people than just for myself. I stepped down from my position because of the simple fact that it could have cost me my early release date. My fellow inmates were getting jealous of my position and could start a fight and get me in trouble.

I couldn't understand what was driving me. The moment I got out of prison, the desire to get high returned immediately. Instead, I went to the Masjid to pray which reminded me how beautiful Islam could be. I had finally found a path to fight my demons. This was the beginning of my leap of faith to Islam. The process was filling the void I ran from for such a long time. It was twenty years of anger, failure, and denial about my plight that had led me here. I felt a sense of relief knowing I had the power to reject the substances that had defined my existence for so long. I found myself overcoming old beliefs that destroyed so much of my character. The pursuit of drugs was no longer my escape from reality in the present and future. I was no longer comfortable with the illusion it provided. I knew I had a Herculean task ahead of me. I prayed for the strength to find my way. I didn't find it. Once again I turned completely to the dark side.

SECOND CONVICTION (7 YEARS).

On September 14, 2010, I stood on the corner of Gates & Marcy higher than a kite straddling a bike, probably worth a few grand. Five police cruisers simultaneously converged on me. Life on my terms was just not working out. My free passes had run out a long time ago. I was placed in handcuffs and seated in the back of a police car until the victim showed up identifying me and her property. I was whacked out of my brain on drugs and almost near death when they apprehended me. My life flashed before my eyes. I had surrounded myself with addicts to make myself feel normal. That way I wouldn't feel like the failure I was. I quickly became the life of the party simply because I had money coming in monthly from my NBA pension. Spending two to three grand at any given time was nothing after a large check came from my NBA pension. This became a regular thing for me and when the check didn't come I boosted. I'd wake up from a coma after smoking for days on end. You could smell the drugs now coming out of my pores, like some kind of exotic stench of a cologne. Who the hell was I fooling? Of course, no one but me. The moment they converged I kept telling myself to leave being a human at the gate until I got home as I knew what faced me ahead. It wasn't like I was living like a human the way I was living, but I had freedom.

Getting busted, while riding to the 79th Precinct, looking out of the window, I saw Mama sitting in front of her building waiting for me where I'd left all of what little I had. When she found out my fate, I knew she'd sell it all with no remorse. I was not aware of my aging, lack of social development, or reality because in my mind I envisioned myself as a flawless individual who saw everybody as wrongdoers and me as right all the time.

When the police arrested me, they threatened me with a mound of evidence I didn't know at the time, they truly did not have. You see, they often lie to get a confession and conviction. Again, they're above the law. A word of advice: never talk to the police without a lawyer. The police even used that age-old scare tactic, "Do you see that tree outside?"

I said, "No."

"Well, there will be one by the time you get out of prison."

I'm sure you've heard the saying, "loose lips sink ships."

I didn't say a word but I was well aware my ship was going down fast. Even the judge told me that if I dared to try to take the case to trial, she would sentence me to the max plus ten years as a persistent felon. With the thought of dying in prison or losing Mama while behind bars, I asked for mercy. I was allowed to speak at the end of the trial after the prosecutor, and then my lawyer spoke. Giving every effort to alter my fate, I stood calmly and spoke slowly at first with my deep voice amplified by the microphone protruding from the Formica table in front of me. My voice seemed to echo off the walls and high ceiling in the courtroom as I made my ultimate request.

"Please, may I hug my mother?"

It was denied. I could only wave and say goodbye. The sorrow and pain on my mother's worn face did not escape me. I was 56 years old and could not fathom dying in prison, which was a very real possibility. My life was in shambles. The judge and the district attorney held all the aces. Even my lawyer told me my ship had sunk. In less than fifteen minutes, my life, every part of it, was now either going to be gone, changed, or packed into boxes. The only real truth that ever came from the police was that there would be a tree outside that window. At least I would get out of prison to see it while it was still small.

At 5:00 a.m., C.O. Evan came to my cell to tell me to pack up. I was on draft for Downstate and to be ready by 8:00 a.m. I would not be allowed a phone call "for security reasons." My second prison sentence was not to be as 'cushy' as my first.

At 8:00 a.m. I walked from Building 5, West 17-upper A side to Building 4 to be processed out. Once there, I was stuffed into a 12-foot by 12-foot cage with 20 other prisoners. There were no benches to sit on so we all had to stand shoulder to shoulder. God forbid you accidentally touch someone! Some of the other felons in that cage with you were murderers and serial killers who would not think twice about killing someone who accidentally bumped into them.

The holding cage was riddled with filth, urine, graffiti, and various gang symbols. There was a toilet without running water, a wall, or a door. The odor coming from it was bad enough to make you vomit. Standing in that cage for nearly an hour, I thought of farm animals, mostly pigs, penned up in their defecation waiting to be loaded onto a truck bound for the slaughterhouse. Finally, my name was called. As I marched out of the cage, my mind and body operated on survival instinct. I knew enough to do exactly as I was told because doing otherwise would get me sprayed in the face with pepper spray and beaten almost to death. I knew because I had seen it happen. The C.Os had the power to do with us as they pleased with no consequence from the law.

In prison, they were the law and I was no longer considered a human being. I felt I was not even considered equal to the shit in the toilet. So then, they shackled my ankles together with a 14-inch chain and lock. The C.O. fitted another chain around my waist tightly with a lock. From there, they hand-cuffed my wrists in front and then secured them to the chain around my waist with yet another lock. By then, I could hardly move and the chains made any thought of escape ineffectual. As though that wasn't enough, the C.O. then chained my right ankle to the left ankle of a much shorter convict. In this situation, I couldn't help wondering to whom I was getting shackled. Is he a serial killer or maybe a schizoid psycho who would get bugged out and therefore get both of us sprayed and beaten? Either way, I would be stuck with him for the next four hours as we boarded the prison transport bus up to Down State Correctional Facility Reception. It was a ride with no talking allowed and windows too high to look out.

The bus ride from Brooklyn Supreme Court was surreal as we passed L.I.U. I watched students milling around campus as we entered the Brooklyn Queens Expressway leading us once again to the notorious Otis Bantum Correctional Center. I was handcuffed to a derelict and I thought to myself, damn, I went from sitting next to Karl Malone to this. I'd become just one of many in the so-called fraternal order of criminals. Swapping war stories and the "I know so and so" talk had me sick to the core. As we approached that big billboard sign that read RIKERS ISLAND before heading onto a connecting little bridge from Elmhurst, Queens to an island of its own, I had a lucid moment. This place could save my life.

The bus was cold most of the way and all I could do to distract myself was think about the past. My first thought went out to the loved ones. I was disappointed and angry about how I was not even allowed to call them before I left for "security reasons." Thinking back about the city that never sleeps, filled with skyscrapers and bright lights, the city that had brought me fame and fortune, I was shaken from my reverie by the smell of cow pastures. I couldn't help myself thinking, "Will I make it back in time to see that tree or will I return in a pine box made from it?" I was preparing myself for the long road ahead with only silence and the occasional clink of a chain.

I looked at the faces of the others seeing my regret as we all tried to cope with possibly losing family members, relationships, and maybe even ourselves. Every mile was like having my life sucked right out of me. Every clinking chain was a reminder that society no longer considered me a human being. The C.O.'s. with their 9-millimeter handguns. Nobody cared I was an ex-NBA player. I was a prisoner with a number. Looking down at my chains, I thought, "My God, what have I done? How could I have let this happen? What will become of me?" Yes, this was the plea deal I accepted.

Four hours of suffering on the bus hog-tied like an animal and left to my thoughts of torment finally ended with my arrival at Downstate Correctional Facility. Escorted off the bus, my shackled ankle partner and I had to penguin waddle to a large holding cage called a Bullpen. The bullpen was even more disgusting than Rikers, with yet another grotesque open, non-functioning toilet. And this time, there were fifty-two inmates crammed in it.

Just before entering the bullpen, a C.O. removed my ankle chains separating me from my bus buddy. After waiting more than an hour, my name was finally called for processing. Handcuffs were removed, and I was placed with my back in front of a white wall. Facing me was a camera and a flamboyant male C.O. Behind him were several male C. Os. and a few very obese female C.Os.

As though I knew what to do the male C.O., bellowed, "Strip and put your clothes in the can." Now standing naked and disgraced, I was told, "Turn, face the wall, bend over, and spread your ass. Now, lift your right foot, now your left. Turn back around and lift your balls. Open your mouth and lift your tongue." The entire time that I was doing as I was commanded the C.O. with the camera was photographing every exposed inch of my body.

From there I was instructed to shower. They gave me and eight other men a portion of whitish-colored liquid to bathe and wash our hair. This liquid was formulated to kill lice, fleas, and any other parasites that might be on our bodies. It smelled identical to pet shampoo and burned my eyes and other sensitive parts of my body. The showers were in one large room with ten shower heads, no privacy, and were even open on two sides allowing C.Os to monitor our every move. Exiting the shower, I picked up my state prison clothes, see-through boxers, paper-thin tee shirts, and button-down green shirts with matching pants. With no surprise, nothing fit. They don't make prison uniforms for people over six feet six inches tall. I was told, "Too bad, deal with it. If you don't like it, don't come to prison." These were two of the most common phrases I heard from every C.O. What I came to realize was that they were right.

I also received one pair of dollar-store sneakers and one pair of black boots, neither of which had any treads and both hurt the sides of my feet. The boots were not insulated, had no padding or insole, and were not waterproof. That meant my feet froze in the winter and got soaked in any kind of snow or rain. The next part of the intake process started with a set of standardized mental health questions. Some of these were, "Have you thought about suicide? Do you want to harm yourself or others? Do you have a pre-existing mental health condition? Do you take any prescribed mental health medications?" In the mix of these questions, the nurse, who was not a mental health professional, asked at least three times if I used drugs or alcohol, and if so, how often. The final set of questions was related to my sexuality; Are you gay? Do you prefer men? Are you transgender? If so, do you have breasts and have you had any type of gender surgery? I came to realize there were many gay and transgender men in prison. Most are flamboyantly open about it and were referred to by inmates and C.Os. as "mooks" or "mukes." Any sexual behavior was strictly forbidden and such behavior with or among mukes is treated as a capital offense.

After having to get dressed in front of everyone, I headed to the barbershop. I was required to cut my fingernails so short that there were hardly any fingernails left. Yes, as you can imagine, it hurt quite a bit. Everyone used the same fingernail clippers. I could only hope I didn't get AIDS, herpes, hepatitis, or God knows what. Then I had to shave with a two-cent disposable razor and cold water. The razor may have worked better had I had shaving cream, but no. This was a prison, so I had to deal with it. The razor cut my skin far better than it cut my facial hair.

Now it was time for the inmate barber to shave all the hair off my head. For this, he used the same trimmers I just watched him use on the other eight inmates ahead of me and the next twenty who would come after me. There was no sense of caution while he was shaving us, much like shearing the wool off a hundred sheep. Just get it done fast and move on to the next. Properly washed and groomed, I waited in another disgusting bullpen with the eight preceding inmates while the other twenty endured their treatments. I guessed about an hour passed when two C.Os. opened the cage door and escorted all of us to yet another cage. This one was much cleaner. We arrived at the Medical Intake Unit.

I had gone too far this time. There was no escaping. It was time to face the music.

My judgment day had come. Carey Scurry, a street legend who could have been an NBA great, sat as an unsung hero in a most dismal prison. I realized the consequences of my addiction in this correctional system whereas I couldn't see it before. I'd tried drug programs: John Luca's program, Palladia, Damon House, J-Cap, and City Bids. Each time I fell back into old habits to the point of being on the run from drug dealers. Growing up I had strong obstacles to overcome, but I could now accept that I was the solitary source of all the suffering in my pitiful life. Rikers had been the strongest therapy yet. I sincerely threw myself into working through the mess I had made of my life. I found that the only thing that could cure anything, apart from death was for me to choose a different way of life. For me, that was Islam.

Rikers Island was one thing, but heading upstate was another. It started at 11:00 a.m. with court callouts. C.O. Canty got word from intake that I was on the pack-up to back up to Ulster. Passing on my radio, sweats, and Puma sneakers to the next man or throwing them out was my option. This was the code of brotherhood that I hadn't had in a while, though I had no idea who would want them. I was hustled into a medium-security prison as I was designated a lesser escape risk and a non-threat to other inmates. After the C.Os secured their weapons, we were escorted to a building secured by a large green metal door. A lieutenant named Fingers appeared from behind that door. He was an old, bald, muscular ex-Attica maximum security prison C.O. on his way out of the system. Dressed in a khaki uniform, he led us into a unit locking the door behind him. The atmosphere was like an intensive care ward.

The new cells were different than the one I was in previously. They were small and spartan, with two concrete beds, a stainless steel sink, and a toilet, with no direct sunlight into the cell. The light was diffused by the plexiglass windows. There was no T.V. and definitely no jailhouse jive talking. The only sound was the clanging of cell doors and an occasional cry for a C.Os assistance. Captain Fingers took each one of us individually into a small room. He sat me in a gray chair and remained standing, listening to his prison radio, concerned about a red dot signal for emergencies such as slashings, or fights. I was slightly confused about why I had been taken from the rest of them.

"Who are you?" he said in a matter-of-fact tone as an introduction.

The feeling of disdain was mutual but I sat motionless and expressionless. Captain Fingers' walkie-talkie gibberish was intrusive in the room. Something told me to just listen to him. His tone softened, "Listen up." His next words were, "This world is a different place. Everybody's snitching, the world around has changed; the life you lived is over; that life doesn't exist anymore."

In hanging with the local thugs recalling how they spoke of snitches, it kicked in that I was being recruited as a snitch. Sensing a glimmer of hope in his new attitude, I said to myself, *It's not over.* I was no snitch. Although I did not say a word, by my body language I wanted him to know that he couldn't disrupt my life or change it and that only I had the power to do that. I was and would never be a snitch. The problem with his procedure of forming allies was nearly everybody in D.O.C. knew who the snitches were. Leaving that room, I felt raped just like that big sign that hung around the facility that read, "Preventing sexual abuse in prison and what inmates need to know." In prison, life was like in the streets. I was told by my OGs to ignore when I see wrong. "The inmates and officers alike will call you a snitch. Labels are the only things that truly follow you in the system, no matter where you go." To avoid these things, I learned to look past wrongdoing; this desensitized and dehumanized me. Prison can disable you; this is what I saw as a new inmate from people with a lot of time in.

This was no dress rehearsal. No holding cell for rehab this time. I was going to the pen for seven years. The news that I was going up north for seven years spread around the old neighborhood like wildfire. Before loading the bus from the Ulster County Prison (UCP) Reception Facility, everybody's head was shaved bald like a military-based discipline to get rid of any lice and to be unable to conceal anything in one's hair. From UCP I was sent to Cape Vincent Correctional Facility in Jefferson County, New York. It's a medium security level facility for 800 plus males and about as far as I could get from the 'hood without being in Canada. In fact, it was so close, that I could see the Canadian landmass ahead from the Cape Vincent Correctional Facility.

— THIRTEEN —

THE MENTAL BREAKDOWN

Being in prison can cause a mental breakdown. It's dehumanizing and generally, inmates can't cope. I did all I could to keep my eye on the prize…getting released, but it was a challenge. The prison doctors and counselors who helped me physically and mentally prepare for the life I truly wanted to live upon my release seemed genuine. Psychiatric doctors mentally brought me to moments of reckoning—to face the demons hiding deep in my psyche—fear, low self-esteem, spiritual bankruptcy, and failure leading to my self-sabotage. I could no longer hide from myself. My life in my eyes had been a total letdown! I had squandered it away. What had I been thinking to throw away such a promising dream? I mean I was one of 210 people who played for the NBA in 1985! How was that a failure? How could I not have seen my glass as full to the brim waiting to flow over?

That was the problem, I wasn't thinking at all! What the psych said rang true. I and only me was responsible for the choices I made.

My disregard, denial, and bad decisions had been what had put me back in jail, somewhere I didn't wish to be. At this point, I had to live with it, good, bad, or indifferent. The consequences I had to face were the results of my final decision to ignore my dire addiction. This time around all I had to do was make better decisions.

See how simple that was. Yeah, maybe for you, but when you're an NBA Legend in your mind, the simplest thing suddenly becomes complicated. Even the small pool of qualified NBA players becomes a noose. You had to perform, you had to win, you had to deliver the man's gold to keep your position. That is hard when all you live with, is doubt. Then there was the situation where everyone wanted a piece of you, if not you- your money. And then there was the ego. Need I say more? And did I not mention that there are levels of addiction? I had no idea when I picked up my first joint that drugs would take me further than I wished to go and keep me longer than I intended to stay! Some people have addiction propensities that can be triggered once they start using. I don't believe anyone wakes up one day and decides that he or she will become an addict, nor are they prepared for what the life of an addict will entail. I was an addict long before I picked up a joint. I was addicted to fear! Here I was already past the halfway mark of life having wasted the best years of my life.

But it's never too late to claim what is yours. For every recovering addict there is a starting point. Although it may take a while, most people would agree that the starting point of recovery comes from a trigger that is greater than the fear of addiction. For me, that day came when I got picked up for the second time and had to spend another seven years in jail. Combined, I had spent twelve years in jail, six times more time than I had been a star on the basketball courts. That was a very sobering realization for me that my being a star was so fleeting and was so very far from the truth. I began to appreciate how many chances I had been given to get my life right and ignored. So many of my friends from before I left for prison, didn't get to live to tell their stories like me. They're dead, plain, and simple.

I got deep into my faith in jail—Islam. It was forbidden to transgress against your brother in faith especially those who have excelled in all aspects of prison life as model prisoners. Instead of fighting the system, they knew the ultimate journey began with redemption only they could embrace. This for me was like having eyes and not being able to see or having ears and not being able to hear until I started using my faculties correctly. In prison, I started to wake up.

While I was using drugs, because I had had poor dental care, my teeth and gums deteriorated. I took advantage of the prison system healthcare and had my teeth replaced. I studied for trade so I would have a skill when I got out. At 56 all I knew how to do was play ball and be an addict. I began taking better care of myself by working out and reading. I embraced my failures and forgave myself for being human. I even congratulated myself for having survived the mean streets of Bed-Stuy.

Getting closer to going home, time seemed to slow down. As my sentence was coming to an end, I knew I would rather die than ever come back to a facility like this. But there is always a positive even in adversity. The prison system had scared me straight.

There were a few weeks to go before my release after being in prison for so many years. Those weeks felt longer than the whole previous seven years. From the wake-up call to pack the pillows, two sheets, and three sets of the green uniform, which I had to pay for if I lost them, to filling out a ten-page fifty questionnaire about my intended whereabouts for my post-release program. I must after being released complete five years of playing it cool on probation to commute my full sentence. I dreaded going back to the environment from which I came but this time I was armed with religious fortitude. I thought of my brother Clifton, whose life had been altered by his experience in jail. He never really recovered and spent his life doing odd jobs. Clifton passed on too early but he did leave behind a beautiful daughter, Mamawwi.

When life showed up and looked me in the eye, I was broken. I no longer had the money I once possessed or had unlimited access to. In debt from borrowing money, I couldn't pay back fast enough, so I moved from addict to criminal. When life showed up, my twenty-year-old daughter from my first relationship was pregnant, and her father was an addict who believed no one else around him knew. My ways and actions were starting to tell on me. And here I was! Minus a few tens of thousands of dollars later, a few shades darker, not knowing the whereabouts of my dentures in a dilemma that lasted for months and it felt like nothing less than an eternity.

— FOURTEEN —

FOURTH QUARTER

REDEMPTION

Without drugs, I found myself wanting to face reality. My attitude had changed. I would live to fight another day. I kept telling myself, "It ain't over 'til it's over." I was here for a reason of that I was sure. I came so close to losing my life countless times but something in me or Allah's grace would not let me leave this world without one last-ditch effort to reclaim the life intended for me. Allah and I were ready for me to have a second chance. Maybe too, Mama, was in the mix for her voice was constantly in my head and my heart. I needed to show her I was the son she had birthed and it was my driver. Though Mama wouldn't live to see me get straight, I know in her heart she believed I would.

Mama didn't deserve all I put her through after all the sacrifices she'd made. And I for damn sure didn't deserve what I had put myself through. My time for fucking up had run way out, and I was on narrow and borrowed time. I wasn't going to be given a no-look pass this time and neither did I want one. Perhaps the worst sin in life I committed was knowing what was right and not doing it. But if you survive hell and back, there comes a time in life when either age or common sense kicks in, and you become so sick and tired of screwing up that you give in to living life on life's terms.

I was released from prison in 2021. With both my arrests I had spent twelve years incarcerated, more years than I had played ball. I often think about where I could have been had I stayed on the path of a striver and a thriver, but that's water under the bridge. Looking back does absolutely nothing. My reality is that I live in Queens, New York in an after-care program facility for people who have been in the penal system. I will be on parole until 2026. My movements and everything I do is monitored. In some ways, I am like a child learning life skills for the first time. Above all, I am determined to *never* be incarcerated again.

Facing my fears head-on, I began to heal. I attended Narcotics and Alcoholics Anonymous, NA/AA to support me in my bid for a second chance of life. The Twelve-step Program was helpful but I believe that a power greater imbued my will to restore my life to sanity. For some people, NA/AA has helped them along the way and I take nothing away from that. I mean, whatever works for you, go for it. It certainly was a part of my recovery but I was focused on getting my mind right. I firmly now believe what James Allen, paraphrasing the book of Proverbs from the King James Bible, "So as a man thinketh, so shall he be."

I wanted to depend on myself and then use all the tools in my recovery arsenal including NA/AA to create the life I now wanted. What makes this piece of the puzzle so important for me is that our belief system in all actuality is the motor core of how we live our lives. I needed to solidify my core. Even Step #2 of the recovery program states that:

> "We came to believe that a Power greater than ourselves can restore us to sanity.
>
> You could put your trust in Christ, Allah, Buddha, but at the end of the day, it will be all up to you."

I am living proof that "All the forces of Darkness cannot stop what God has ordained." (Isiah 14: 27). All I need to add to that equation now is my fortitude.

I believe that Allah is the God of my understanding who has allowed me to recover, restore, and restart my life, however little life I have left. I would live for Him and I fully embraced Islam. My faith in a higher power is deeper and stronger than ever. I practice mindfulness and gratitude. I wake up at 4:00 a.m. each morning for my daily prayers to help me through my day.

Here is what I learned from the school of hard knocks…hell from flat-out TKO punches. When faced with a problem that seems greater than yourself:

1. Instead of giving up, call someone or look deep within.
2. Remember the pain and refuse to go backward.
3. Do what adults are supposed to do. Grow up
4. It is better not to make a vow than to make a vow and not keep it.
5. Never let go of the hand of God.
6. Know your journey here on this earthly plain is for a reason; you might not understand it but it is taking you to where you belong.
7. When you get knocked down. Get up.
8. Your thoughts are powerful…mind what you think.

9. You are in control of your heaven and hell.
10. Mistakes are a human dynamic. Forgive yourself.
11. For me, this one is really important. It is in losing yourself that you often find yourself.
12. Be grateful for the gift you were given. Try not to squander it away.
13. If you are not grounded in who you are Money will show you who you are not supposed to be.

— FIFTEEN —
THE PLEDGE

Believe in a higher power. If that's what it takes to stay drug-free, I got this. Granted, it takes a helluva lot more than a higher power, it takes you. If you remember, I believed in (Allah) or Islam while I was still getting high. So, what's the difference now? What makes me more serious than ever before about staying healthy and drug-free? ME! Who am I was the question I needed to answer?

God gives every man, woman, and child a gift or talent. What you do with it is entirely up to you. My talent was basketball. Despite poverty and my environment, I had all of the tools I needed growing up in Bedford Stuy. When I'd set my sights on basketball, as hard and as challenging as it was, I did not allow anything to deter me from accomplishing my goal of playing pro basketball. Basketball gave me the life I envisioned but my choices turned my gift into a living hell. My pride, my ego, my lack of discipline in my personal life, and my attitude of flaunting what I had and living up to other's expectations took me down a path of destruction. By the time I knew that I was an addict, I was powerless over my addiction. But it's never too late unless you make that choice.

How my recovery all started was with me admitting that I was powerless and that my life had become unmanageable. This was very hard for me to do, even as I literally ended up chasing death. The insane part was smoking was supposed to have given me a heart attack, and still, I went on and on. When I started losing myself, the things I sacrificed…money, family, career, everything, for this shit was what I settled for. Crack made me not want to give a fuck.

I think we all pledge something at some point in our lives. For some, it may be a pledge to religion or maybe a life of honesty and kindness. Others pledge themselves to the streets and their gangs. No matter what pledge one makes, it comes with a code of loyalty, or at least it used to. I have chosen not to continue with my prison story. I think you get the picture and I pray it has scared you straight. My advice to any young reader who chooses to commit a crime is don't do it! Think twice. This book is my cautionary tale.

My pledge today is to grab that second chance life has given me and to show myself that everything my mother and grandmother believed about me was true…I was and am special even with a dark past. I also pledge to pay forward all I can through my non-profit organization, A Hoopsters Journey.

I have served my time. I am clean and now lead a productive life. I strive to be a kinder more gentle person to my family and everyone around me. I coach kids through my nonprofit, A Hoopster's Journey. I have been honored to speak about my life and I'm willing to share my story with kids in the inner city and beyond. I recently spoke at the Bard Micro College for Just Community Leadership and am working on film projects to make up for lost time.

— SIXTEEN —

LIFE METAPHORICALLY THROUGH BASKETBALL

If, as they say, I chose my incarnation to learn lessons only life can teach, this has been a difficult life. The beauty of life though is that one has choices. Not staying trapped in a previous choice is a decision you can make at any time. Transforming oneself beyond the straight and narrow confines of our small egos requires going beyond human obsession. It took facing death for me to dig deep inside my soul and reclaim what Mama had planted there from the time I was born. My Mama always instilled in me that, "Hard work pays off." Using your whole self, which is the team, to win the game as well as to score. If the ball doesn't rotate, you are not utilizing your full potential.

My Superman dream was brought to its knees by my kryptonite—drugs. Like basketball, recovery isn't a one-man game; it's a team game. Life metaphorically through the lens of basketball is the same as on the court. Your teammates become your second family. In life you should, like in basketball, have two Guards, two Forwards, and one Center. You should also be prepared to understand that the game of life is like basketball, 85% mental and 15% physical. The Rim is 18 inches, and the ball is 14 inches in circumference so it might bounce, spin, rotate, and go in or not. Gravity and simple science are the key factors in life on and off the court. But, if the Shooting Guard is open, you might get a 3-pointer from the perimeter. A loose ball, a steal, an assist, or a slam dunk, is the icing on the cake, the nail in the coffin. It's an almost guaranteed basket.

    The Center is the core of the team. He rebounds and sets the pace, protecting the home, which is the basket. Defense is the name of the game, keeping your opponent from advancing. Your opponent in life could be substance abuse, self-defeating behaviors, poverty, etc. Usually, this role of defense is filled by your immediate family. They have your best interest at heart so pay attention to their concerns. Instead of running to my family for support, I ran away from them. This was a bad move. I dropped the ball. Family can provide the defense you need to rebound from life's hardships and you will eventually win. Scoring is a plus, being responsible, being a good citizen, being a team player, these are the points you need to score in the game of life.

    Then you have your Power Forward who is the enforcer. He advocates and influences the structure of the court. He is the first line of the offense who sets the tone of the game after your center. Your Power Forward, being your core value, is your ambition. Without him involved, the opposition, the demons could steal the ball and score, so if you are playing against addiction and adversity in life, they could repeat the destruction you inflict on yourself. My power forward also happened to be in my family. My brothers Dale and Paul were two powerful Power Forwards who steered me to use my gift which landed me as a draft pick. Like with my core, I abandoned my power forwards and as a result, I also abandoned myself.

The Point Guard is a means of viewing life itself. You're dealing with a clock and you have to see the fast breaks life grants you, sometimes. It's not in your best interest to launch the ball before your Small Forward is ready to score. The opposition could easily steal the ball and go on a fast break, which is the easy way, so to speak, in life. I had many point guards in my life from the people on the street who looked out for me, to my teammates who tried to coral my ways, to my agent Joe and John Lucas who gave me a big break the first time I went to rehab. I failed to see the fast breaks they offered and took for granted that they would always be there. When I was too far gone for help even my point guard had to stand down.

So, in many ways, basketball parallels life in general. Once the Point Guard crosses half-court, he enters the realm of opportunity. You have the choice now to explore the different possibilities. Things are clearer and you begin to see the fruits of your labor. The scoreboard is usually at half-court. There are two sides to every decision you make, you get what you want or you don't. When the play is being executed, you need to be aware of your surroundings. On teams, you might have slow strong players or weak fast players, and knowing the components of the team determines your success as a player, a teammate, and ultimately a human being. Once the Point Guard views the floor, he gets the ball to the Small Forward or Shooting Guard.

During my career, I played as a Small Forward. A lot of expectations are put on Small Forwards: some of the greats like LeBron James, Larry Bird, and Scottie Pippen played this position. Their job was to score. The weight of the team is on their shoulders. They are the final goal of execution.

To score in life, you are rewarded simply for positive behavior and results by trial and error. But with a criminal mindset, you will likely lose. You have to balance the playing floor. An open jump shot is reminiscent of one's plans and dreams coming together all in one motion.

My advice to any young reader who chooses to commit crimes is don't do it! This book is my cautionary tale. It's all about being purely honest with oneself. It's about the harmony of mind, body, and soul. You're leading towards the heavens and raining down in victory. It's one of the most glorifying feelings in the world, even better than getting drafted or playing for your hometown Knicks.

— SEVENTEEN —
THE AFTERMATH

Here is the thing about life…everyone is connected. My behavior did not just affect me it affected everyone my life touched and I can only hope and pray that some of the damage I created can be undone or repaired. I was fifty-six years old the last time I went to prison. Mama died in 2021 and she never saw me get clean. She saw me as an NBA and international star with enormous promise for which I am grateful and she witnessed my demise, aberrant behavior, and prison time. I've worked hard to forgive myself for that especially since she always believed in me. So many people had gone on with their lives and here at sixty-one years old I was starting over but after a long period of being lost, I found the strength to go on and the humility to ask for forgiveness. Now I have started making amends to all the people I hurt and hope they can find it in their hearts to forgive me.

Doris is married and has a new family. Our son, Kaleef, now 41 years old lives in the Bronx where he works as a fashion designer. We speak and we're slowly building a father/son relationship and getting to know each other. Doris and I sometimes speak as well.

Brenda Benton was one of the women I had a relationship with who bore me a son, Jareem. I was never in his life and he has borne the scars of my transgressions. Jareem and I speak. He is in a rehab facility in Georgia. If only I had a do-over.

Once a Scurry, always a Scurry. My brothers and sisters never stopped trying to help me get clean. Like me, both Willie, who played for New Hampshire College, and Moses, from The University of Las Vegas played college basketball though neither went pro. Moses lives in Las Vegas and works for Delta Airlines. Willie works for the government in Manchester, NH. My brother Clifton and my sister Eddie Ruth are deceased. My brother Paul has his own afterschool program in Brooklyn and Dale is a retired correction officer. My sister Gina works for the City of NY and Linda is a retired schoolteacher.

My wife of ten years, Cassandra, who after trying so hard to save me finally got a divorce. She remarried and did a great job raising our children. Kayla is now thirty-two years old and is a hairstylist in Flatbush, Brooklyn. We have a good relationship. Dayna is 30 and a medical technician in Flatbush as well. We are earnestly working on our relationship and I feel I am in a good place with her.

I am now 61 years old and clean…no drugs or alcohol! I have a new attitude toward life, my family, and the people around me. I am trying to show them I have rehabilitated myself and will stay on the straight and narrow path of redemption. Now acknowledging I have disappointed a lot of people, I know I have a long way to go to revive and reconstruct the family relationships that were and are important to me. I practice self-care, and self-compassion and continually challenge negative thoughts. To that end, my energies are totally focused on motivational speaking, and I take enormous pride in the initiative I have taken to develop my non-profit, A Hoopster's Journey, LLC. The nonprofit is supported by Game Over by Eric Hicks, the NBA Retired Player's Association, and community donations. I've dedicated my life to A Hoopster's Journey with the mission of engaging inner-city youth through sports and acting as a role model to encourage staying in schools, avoiding drugs, and staying out of prison.

ACKNOWLEDGEMENTS

Of course, I acknowledge Mama for giving me life and all she toiled to give me. I also thank Grandma Ruth for helping Mama raise me. I am now becoming the man you oped I would be, RIP.

In a commitment to my new outlook on life, I thank my sisters and brothers, Clifton, Linda, Dale, Paul, Carolyn (Gina), Moses, and Willie (Tiny). And to Clifton and Eddie Ruth, RIP.

To my children Kaleef, Jareem, Kayla, Dayna…I want to get to know you and for you to know the new me.

To Doris, Sandy, Brenda, and Liza…I appreciate you all more than you know.

To Uncle Andrew, you were like a father to me, RIP.

To Aunt Janie, you are a second mother.

To Coach Arthur Wachtel, you saw our potential and was the founder of "The Scurry Brothers."

To my High School Coach, Ray Haskins for developing my game.

A shout out to my Long Island University teammates…you know who you are and I'll never forget you.

To the NBA and the NBA Retired Players Association…with deep gratitude, I honor you.

To my Agents Earl Monroe, Alan Herman, and Joe Glass, thank you for your guidance and assistance in my growth and development as a player.

To my fellow players, Karl Malone, Mark Eaton, John Stockton, Thurl Bailey, Adrian Dantley, Rickey Greene, and Darrell Griffith (Dr. Dunkenstein), I honor you all.

To Dr. J (Julius Erving) for giving me a secret tip on how to be a better player when I was in high school.

To my friend Eric Cousar, tried and true.

To Eric Hicks, Idris Conry, Kelvin Pompey, and TD Bank for believing in me and supporting A Hoopster's Journey, LLC, my nonprofit. I shall make you proud!

And to Tra'von Williams for introducing me to Wordeee and Patrice Samara, who never lost faith in me. She persevered and guided me in telling my story by helping to set a new high standard for myself and my behavior. I am eternally grateful.

Above all, I thank ALLAH for protecting me from what I thought I wanted and blessing me with what I didn't know I needed. I praise ALLAH for beneficence and generosity. I'm so grateful for each day you have given me.

I have a deep respect for my family and the people who care and cared about me.

www.ingramcontent.com/pod-product-compliance
Lightning Source LLC
Chambersburg PA
CBHW051615010526
44107CB00037B/1442/J